MURDER O...

Veteran Broadway producer Max Marsden hired his old friend Julian Quist, the top public relations expert, to help promote *Queen Bee*, an up-coming musical. Advance sales were healthy; the problem was Sharon Ladd, the Hollywood superstar who headed the cast. The temperamental Miss Ladd threatened the whole venture with her unexplained absences from rehearsals, her temper tantrums on stage.

Sharon's love life and her five marriages had made headlines for almost two decades. And she was not only beautiful, she was a brilliant comedienne. Without her, *Queen Bee* was finished. Unfortunately, before Quist could find out what her problem was, she was arrested for murder. According to the police, Sharon and her ex-husband, Leon Zuckerman, a famous producer, had entered the hotel lobby at the same time, and had had a flaming row in front of a crowd of fascinated spectators. Then a few hours later, she had gone to his suite and shot him three times. Drugs as well as the murder gun were found in her room.

Motive, weapon, opportunity—it was a solid circumstantial case. Sharon swore, however, that she never took drugs and that she had not gone near Zuckerman or his hotel suite. Quist believed her, but how could he prove that she was innocent? Where could he find a lead to the unknown enemy who had framed her? She could be the next victim of a psychotic killer, and, Quist was warned, so could he.

MURDER OUT OF WEDLOCK

A Julian Quist Mystery Novel

by

Hugh Pentecost

ROBERT HALE · LONDON

ISBN 0 7090 1827 4

Robert Hale Limited
Clerkenwell House
Clerkenwell Green
London EC1R 0HT

Printed in Great Britain by
St Edmundsbury Press, Bury St Edmunds, Suffolk
and bound by Hunter & Foulis Limited

PART ONE

1 "When you've invested several million dollars of your friends' money and your own," Max Marsden said, "you don't want to see it all go down the drain because of some crazy, irresponsible dame."

"Several *million* dollars?" Julian Quist said, showing his surprise.

"Fifty years ago, when I started, you could put on a Broadway musical for a few thousand dollars," Marsden said. "Now it runs into the millions. That's why you and your friends are paying thirty-five to fifty dollars for a ticket to spend a couple of hours in the theater."

"Telephone numbers," Quist said.

"I'll show you a production budget for *Queen Bee* if I can get you interested," Marsden said.

Quist grinned at him. "You want me to invest?"

"I want you to save my investment," Marsden said. "You're the only person I know, Julian, who might be able to persuade an egotistical bitch with a star complex to get back on the rails and keep a lot of us from drowning in our own blood!"

The two men were talking together in Julian Quist's private office at Julian Quist Associates, one of the top public relations firms in the country. Max Marsden, a shaggy, gray-haired man in his late sixties, a permanently unlighted

3

cigar in one corner of his mouth, looked somehow out of place in the very mod office, with its chromium-plated armchairs that surprised you by being comfortable when you sat in them, surrounded by a collection of Chuck Hinman's shaped canvases which Quist had hanging there that day. Quist, thirty years younger than his friend, was blond, handsome as a Greek god on an old coin, elegantly dressed in a tropical worsted summer suit. Quist's secretary had brought them coffee and sandwiches.

Marsden's visit had been unexpected, but when Quist had first come to New York fifteen years ago his first chance was given to him by Max Marsden, famous theatrical producer, as assistant to the publicity director for a Broadway show. Quist had gone on to build his own reputation, establish his own firm, but he had never forgotten Max Marsden's early help, and he was available to this old friend at any time, day or night.

"So let's get down to facts, Max," Quist said.

Marsden moved his unlighted cigar from one corner of his mouth to the other. He glanced at his coffee mug, saw that it was empty, and put it down on the glass-topped table beside his chair. "I haven't produced anything on Broadway for nearly four years, Julian. At today's costs you have to really love something to run the risks. Then this property, *Queen Bee*, came my way. It's based on a novel by George Hendrix. You've read it?"

Quist shook his head.

"A fantasy," Marsden said. "A woman from somewhere in outer space comes to Earth, takes on all the powerful men, and beats them at their own game. Feminists loved it and made the novel a best seller. What came to me was a musical version; a marvelous musical score by Jerry Heston, a book and lyrics by Henry Thatcher. Biggest names in the business. Multiple sets, illusions of flying in space. I was hooked, but it was obviously going to be astronomically

4

expensive. Too big a risk to run, but somehow I couldn't shake it." He made an impatient gesture. "If you wanted to hire the most glamorous woman in show business who would you think of?"

"A film star?"

"Yes, because there isn't a Broadway name big enough to carry it. I had to have someone the whole damned country would want to pay to see."

"So you got Sharon Ladd, glamorous, notorious, the sex symbol of the eighties."

"Yes, God help me," Marsden said. "I went to Holly-wood, twisted her arm, made her an offer she couldn't refuse. Twenty-five thousand dollars a week, ten percent of the gross, five percent of the profits."

"Wow!" Quist said.

"It's not a world's record," Marsden said. "I understand Richard Burton got somewhere around sixty thousand a week plus for his run in *Camelot*. In any case, when I got Sharon I had the bait for up-front money. I got backers, put in my own money, which I've never done before, and we were, I thought, under way."

"I heard you were starting previews next Monday," Quist said.

"Maybe, just maybe," Marsden said. "Joe Philbin is han-dling the public relations. He's sold us theater parties and advance box office in a big way. We've got it made—if we have a show."

"Because Sharon Ladd is not doing what?" Quist asked.

"Sometimes, during rehearsals, she has been just mar-velous," Marsden said, "everything we ever dreamed of. I watch her in one of those moments and I have visions of money pouring in at the box office for the next five years, investors paid back and raking in the profits. The next day she doesn't show up at all with no explanations, no warn-ing, not even a phone call. The next day she is so bombed

5

out with booze she can't walk across the stage, screaming at the other actors, the orchestra leader, the director. You'd have to ring down the curtain and refund everyone's mone̸ if she turned up for a show that way. Then there are th̸ ͡ays when she shows up and is just nothing—no vital-̸ , can't sing or dance, can't remember the words or ͡usic. Like a zombie." Marsden shuddered, as if he'd remembered a nightmare.

"So you fire her and get yourself another girl," Quist suggested.

"There is no 'other girl,'" Marsden said. "We'd have to refund a million bucks in party sales and other advances. We can't; that money's spent."

"Complain to Equity," Quist said.

"Disciplines, rebukes, warnings aren't going to get the show on the road."

"You've checked out with the people she's worked for in Hollywood? After all, she's the biggest star in the business, Max. You don't get there playing now-you-see-me-now-you-don't."

"I sometimes wonder," Max said, his voice bitter. "I sit up at night looking at some of her old films. Is she an actress or is she famous just because she's been married five times and had more lovers than you can count on your fingers and toes?"

"And—?"

"She's damned good, or she can be made to look damn good by a top director. She always has had top directors, including Leon Zuckermann, who was married to her briefly."

"There's a key difference between film acting and stage acting," Quist said. "In films you shoot a scene until you get it right and then it's in the can, finished, you can forget it. On stage you do the same thing over and over, night after night, matinee after matinee. Some actors get bored be-

6

yond endurance doing the same thing again and again, world without end."

"Not a real professional. Sharon has been pampered and catered to and spoiled for far too long, I guess." Max twisted in his chair. "When she's good I'm reminded of a star you have probably seen on the late show—Carole Lombard. Sharon is beautiful, vital, a brilliant comedienne, everything that could make *Queen Bee* a smashing success. How to keep her that way?"

Quist was silent for a moment. "Just what do you expect me to do, Max?"

"I don't know, Julian. But dealing with complicated and temperamental people is your business. Spend some time with her and you might find the right button to press. But it's got to be quick, friend. We're running out of time."

"You hire me to beef up public relations and she'd have to give me some time. I don't want to step on Joe Philbin's toes. He's done a great PR job for you, and he was my boss and my friend when I first worked for you."

"I can explain to Joe why you're really on board," Max said. "And I can't afford to hire you, Julian. I'm asking this as a favor to a friend."

Quist laughed, pushed back his chair, and stood up. "I couldn't be hired to deal with a temperamental lady, but as a favor to a friend. . . ? You've got it, Max. Now, let's discuss ways and means."

The Tempest Theater is just west of Broadway in the mid-forties, one of Manhattan's larger playhouses used almost exclusively for musicals. It had once had a reputation for marvelous acoustics, but in today's musical theater that hardly mattered, with voices and music both electronically amplified.

A uniformed security guard had let Quist into the theater from the lobby. He stood at the back of the darkened auditorium looking down at the brilliantly lighted stage where a non-musical scene was in rehearsal. There were a dozen people scattered around in the audience seats watching a beautiful blond woman and a handsome young man working on stage. Sitting in the last row of seats was someone Quist knew from past exploitation work for plays, Larry Shields, Broadway's top director of musicals. Max Marsden had gone for only the best in his expensive production of *Queen Bee*.

Quist could hear Martin Powell, the leading man, loud and clear as he and Sharon Ladd moved through the scene being rehearsed, but Sharon Ladd appeared to be sleepwalking and Quist couldn't hear a word she spoke.

"I can't hear you, Sharon!" Larry Shields called out from just in front of Quist.

The blonde turned to face out, and she was suddenly quite alive, eyes bright, her scarlet mouth an angry slit. "So move down closer!" she called out, quite clearly.

"This is where you have to be heard," Shields told her.

"So, when there are some paying customers out there they'll hear me!"

In that angry moment Sharon Ladd was very much alive. Quist saw that, as Max Marsden had said, she did indeed bear a striking resemblance to the late, lovely Carole Lombard.

"Hold it!" Larry Shields called out, and started down the aisle toward the stage.

"Do we have to spend all day on this puking piece of junk?" Sharon called out to him.

Someone had moved in the semi-darkness at the rear of the house to stand beside Quist. It was Joe Philbin, Max's promotion man and an old friend of Quist's, his first boss when he'd worked for Max fifteen years ago.

"Our charming leading lady rides the waves," Philbin said.

8

The two men shook hands warmly.

"Max told you why I'm here, Joe?" Quist asked.

"I offer my condolences," Philbin said. "The only way you can light a fire under that lady is, I suspect, in bed!"

"I am otherwise engaged," Quist said. Joe Philbin, an old friend, didn't have to be told that Quist was referring to Lydia Morton, who shared his Beekman Place apartment with him.

"How is Lydia?" Philbin asked.

"In fine form, as always," Quist said.

"Give her my best."

"Will do. What is it with Sharon Ladd, Joe?"

Philbin shrugged. "I wish to God I could tell you, Julian. There are moments when she takes your breath away, she's so good. Then she's like this, or not here at all, or drunk as your problem uncle."

"She's a pro," Quist said. "She's drawing top money, she's got a fabulous script, according to Max, thousands of people can't wait to pay to see her. What more could she ask? She has to care about her reputation as a performer."

"Says who?" Philbin asked. "So Max has hired you to find out what's wrong. The old boy is up a very deep creek if he can't get her straightened out."

"He hasn't hired me for anything, Joe. I'm not muscling in on you. I agreed to try something as a favor to Max."

"If you don't *have* to get involved with our Sharon," Philbin said, "I'd try running something under a four-minute mile to get away from her."

"I promised Max," Quist said. "So, when there's a break, can you take me backstage to meet her? Just tell her I'm helping with public relations."

"May the Lord watch over you," Philbin said.

Larry Shields, the director, spent some time talking to the two actors on stage; then he turned, his face flushed with anger, and called out to the scattering of people in the audience section: "We're taking a fifteen-minute break!"

He stalked up the aisle and out the back of the theater.

"Bar just across the street," Joe Philbin said. "She's driving him to drink."

"Chance for you to introduce me," Quist said.

They walked down the aisle, up onto the stage, and back of the set toward the dressing room area.

"Would you believe Max built a whole new dressing room for his star on the stage level? Dressing room, shower and bath, oriental rug, a rest room with a bed in it. That's where I understand the lady does her best work." Philbin knocked on the door which sported a gold embossed sign that said "Miss Ladd."

A woman's voice called out. "If it's anything more from that bastard Shields, I'm not in!"

"It's Joe Philbin, Miss Ladd."

"Oh, Joe! Just a minute."

A key turned in the lock and a dark-haired woman in a plain black dress over which she wore a full-length Dutch apron opened the door.

"Hi, Janet," Philbin said. He introduced Quist. "Janet Lane, Sharon's personal dresser—Julian Quist, who's going to help promote the show."

"Not a good time, Mr. Philbin," Janet Lane said.

"Come on in, Joe," Sharon Ladd called from beyond in what Quist saw was a rather elegant suite of rooms. "You hear all that baloney out front?"

The lovely Sharon Ladd was sitting at her dressing table, facing a mirror surrounded by colored light bulbs. She saw her guests in the mirror and turned. This was not the "zombie" Quist had seen on stage. She was electrically alive, eyes bright, smile inviting. Her interest seemed to be centered on Quist. Philbin introduced them.

"I didn't know Joe needed help," she said. "From what

I've heard he's sold dozens of theater parties, a big advance."

"My job is to do a special promotion on you, personally, Miss Ladd," Quist said.

"I didn't know I needed that," Sharon said. "God knows there's enough juicy gossip printed about me without hiring someone to add to it."

"I think Max wants to get away from gossip and spread some truths about a really great star," Quist said.

"The truth about me?" She laughed, and it was musical. "That might close the show, Mr. Quist. And since you're going to work that intimately with me, it's Sharon—Julian."

He was looking past her to the dressing table, where five photographs of five men were standing against the base of the mirror.

"My rogues' gallery," Sharon said. "My five ex-husbands. I keep them here to remind me not to be a damn fool again."

Quist was aware that the lady was making a very careful appraisal of him.

"There isn't time now to go into my dark history," Sharon said. "As soon as Shields gets over being outraged with me we'll be called back. Rehearsal is supposed to be over at six o'clock, unless that bastard decides to keep us all night."

"Where are you staying in town, Sharon?" Quist asked.

"The Hotel Beaumont," Sharon said. "But there's no point in trying to talk to me there. I can't even walk across the lobby without being swamped by ghouls who would like to strip my clothes off."

Quist knew he should have guessed she would be staying at New York's top luxury hotel. "Actually the Beaumont's just a couple of blocks from where I live on Beekman Place," he said. "I can provide you with a home-cooked dinner at seven o'clock if you say the word. There'll be no rubberneckers there."

Sharon's smile widened. "It's a date," she said.

"And if Shields keeps you late—"

"If I have a date with you, Julian," the lady said, "I'll be on time. If Shields gets cantankerous I'll just walk out on him! I'm still that important!"

If you want gossip or solid information about people in the theater or films, the place to go for it in New York is the Players on Gramercy Park. Almost a century ago Edwin Booth, the great actor of his time, had given his private home, the interior designed by the legendary Stanford White, as a club for actors. Being a wise man, Booth had suggested that the club should be open to men in the other arts and so-called men of the theater. Booth's theory was that a club that only admitted actors would find its members only willing to talk about themselves to people who only wanted to talk about themselves. Quist, often a promoter of theater projects, had been a member for about ten years. He enjoyed dropping in there, talking with the greats and near-greats of all the arts, and he had found that the Walter Hampden Memorial Library, housed on the club's second floor, was a gold mine of information about the kind of people he was so often hired to promote.

Leaving the Tempest Theater, Quist headed downtown to the club to find someone who could provide him with something of Sharon Ladd's background. He walked into the bar and grill at the Players just after noon and realized that this was his lucky day. Sitting at a round table in a corner of the room, sipping a glass of orange juice, was a handsome, gray-haired man who was an old friend. Ian Moss, British born, had been lured to Hollywood some fifty years ago, and had appeared in so many films that he was as well known to most Americans as an old family friend. He had been nominated for a half dozen Academy

12

Awards as "best supporting actor," never won one, but was respected and loved by all the people who had worked with him over the years. Quist joined him at the round table.

"If it isn't too early, Ian, I'll buy you the drink of your choice if you'll talk to me for half an hour," he said.

"Julian, how nice to see you," the old actor said in his deep, mellifluous voice. He lifted his orange juice. "But this is breakfast, along with the coffee and toast the waiter is about to bring me. But I don't need a bribe to enjoy the pleasure of talking with you. Sit down."

Quist sat down across the table from his friend. "Max Marsden has hired me to give him a hand with his new musical," he said.

"Poor Max," Ian Moss said.

"You've heard he's got trouble?"

"Everyone in the theater who's got ears to hear knows he's got trouble," Moss said. "How are you supposed to help him?"

"Figuratively, to spank Sharon Ladd's behind and get her to functioning like a professional," Quist said.

"Before it's too late?"

"Precisely."

The old actor put down his emptied juice glass as the waiter brought him coffee and a covered dish of hot buttered toast. "Even St. Francis could have attacked a lion who was too much for him," he said.

"In this case a lioness," Quist said, grinning at his friend.

Moss poured coffee into his cup from a silver pot. "The most dangerous, the female of the species," he said.

"You ever work with her, Ian?"

Moss's dark eyes looked at Quist out of their deep pouches. There was a twinkle of humor in them. "Just twenty-two years ago I was hired to play a character role in Sharon's first film. She was just seventeen years old. That will give you an idea about her age—and mine." Moss

13

sipped his coffee. "It wasn't much of a film. I don't even remember the title, though you could find it upstairs in the library if it matters."

"I want to know about the woman, Ian, not her theatrical history. I want to know how to get at her."

"If you'll pardon a vulgarity," Moss said. "I would suggest you try unzipping your fly."

"As you very well know," Quist said, "I'm what you might call 'otherwise engaged.'"

"How is that dear Lydia of yours?"

"Fine."

"Does she know you've taken on Sharon Ladd as a project? Because if she does, she'd better arm herself with a shotgun. If our Sharon fixes her sights on you, Julian, she won't let the great Jehovah stand in her way."

"Tell me about the real woman and not the games she plays," Quist said.

Moss lifted the silver lid off his plate of toast, looked at what was there, and replaced it. A frown creased his wrinkled forehead. "I suddenly remember that name of that ghastly film," he said. "*Little Miss Fauntleroy*. I played the counterpart of the crotchety old grandfather that C. Aubrey Smith played opposite Freddie Bartholemew in *Little Lord Fauntleroy* longer ago than I like to remember. Some nonsense about a Brooklyn girl who inherits a British title. It was hogwash, but it launched a startling career— Sharon's. Career as an actress and career as a sensational sex symbol."

"Which came first with her?" Quist asked.

"Actress," Moss said. "She worked hard, she studied with the best teachers. She learned from doing. She was lucky after that first piece of junk in getting a few good ones. After she'd made it big, she made her own choices and she never guessed wrong. Not a bomb in a carload."

"But her behavior at work? Was she hard to handle?"

14

Moss shrugged. "Actors who have worked with her have nothing but good things to say about her. Producers, directors, writers and business associates would have a different story. Absurd demands, special privileges. I understand Max has spent about ten thousand dollars to build her a new dressing room at the Tempest."

"You should see it," Quist said. "Incidentally, she has five photographs of her ex-husbands on her dressing table. To remind her not to be a damn fool again, she told me."

Moss nodded. "Even twenty years ago the big moguls in Hollywood fought to protect their stars from scandal. Link a woman star's name with a man and she'd better marry him or else. Today it doesn't matter. Women stars have illegitimate babies and nobody cares. Sharon? She was sex-crazy, I think. Maybe the studios pressured her into marriage. Just maybe she dreamed of something permanent, when sexually and psychologically it wasn't possible for her."

"Why would she take this job with Max and then deliberately screw it up?" Quist asked. "You say actors respect her, like working with her. She's threatening a whole cast the way she's behaving at the Tempest."

"It's somehow out of key for her," Moss said. "Maybe she knows that when the time comes she can pull it off."

"Max and Joe Philbin tell me that there have been moments when she's just wonderful in this show."

"She's a big talent and a big ego," Moss said. He smiled. "Maybe someone in the show has said 'no' to her offer of sexual delights. Marty Powell, her leading man, is happily married, two lovely kids. He could have told her to go peddle her papers. Larry Shields, her director, is a man with a lot of vitality and drive."

"They're in a head-on collision course at the moment," Quist said.

"That in itself could be a kind of sexual excitement,

15

couldn't it, Julian? I'm a little old to remember how that was. Or," and a twinge of pain crossed his face, "is it just that I spent fifty-six years with one woman and never once thought of anyone else."

Quist remembered that Ian Moss had lost his lifetime wife only about a year ago.

"There is someone who might be able to give you a more intimate picture of Sharon than I can," Moss said. "Bud Tyler."

"The racing car driver?"

"And Sharon's last husband," Moss said.

"My God, I'd forgotten. Wasn't he in some kind of smash-up?"

"Big stock-car race down in the Carolinas somewhere," Moss said. "Terrible burns, paralyzed from the waist down. Happened after he and Sharon had been divorced for about a year. The way I hear it, Julian, she paid all his medical bills, probably supports him to this day."

"Then there is a human side to her," Quist said.

Moss shrugged. "Could be. Could also be some kind of legal settlement. I don't know."

"Well, I can't go to Carolina to find him," Quist said.

"No need to," Moss said. "There was a piece about him in the paper a few months back. He lives somewhere here in the Village, I think. Charles Tyler. Bud was a sort of professional nickname. Probably find him in the phone book."

Charles Tyler was in the phone book. Quist decided against calling the man to ask for an appointment. That way he could avoid a "no" for an answer. He did make a call, however, to his office, where he talked with Lydia Morton.

Lydia is a striking auburn-haired woman who looks more like a high-fashion model than the brilliant writer and re-

16

searcher for Julian Quist Associates that she is. She is more than that to Quist. They have lived together for a number of years now, and the love between them binds them closer than any legal ties could have done. Why no marriage?

"Because it's so perfect we don't want to change one single detail of it," Quist told friends who'd had the temerity to ask.

"We're having America's sex queen for supper," Quist told Lydia, "if you don't mind, luv."

"I always enjoy evenings alone with you," Lydia said.

"I know you are America's sex queen, but you haven't earned the title, and if you ever try I'll wring your lovely neck. We're having Sharon Ladd, if you don't mind whipping up a little something."

"Julian!"

Quist chuckled. "I love you," he said.

"Wouldn't you prefer to take that great lady out to some fancy place?" Lydia asked.

"No way. We'd be surrounded by fans and autograph hounds and what have you. Sharon would be putting on a show for them instead of me."

"You need a show put on for you?"

"Oh, come on, luv!" Quist said. "I'm doing a favor for Max. I want to find out why Sharon Ladd is making so much trouble for him. Max can be hurt where it hurts the most."

"In the pocketbook?" Lydia asked.

"Smart girl," Quist said. "I asked the lady for seven o'clock—but rehearsal could string out. Can you dream up something that will stay warm in a double boiler?"

"Yes, Master!" Lydia said. "Mine not to reason why—!"

Quist located the place where Charles "Bud" Tyler lived. It was in an old brownstone, remodeled into small apartments, on Jane Street in the Village. The name plates outside the front door indicated "Tyler, 1R." Quist rang the bell. After a short delay there was the clicking sound that permitted Quist to open the front door and step inside. He walked to the rear of the hall and knocked on the apartment door there.

"Come in! The door isn't locked," a man's voice called out.

Quist went in and found himself in a small living room, the walls plastered with pictures of racing cars, drivers in helmets and goggles. Bud Tyler was still living with his past. At the far end of the room was a door leading out into a small garden. The figure of a man in a wheelchair appeared there.

"Oh!" the man in the wheelchair said. "I'd ordered something from the local deli. I thought you were the delivery boy. Who the hell are you?"

Quist fought back the shock he felt. The man in the wheelchair had, almost literally, no face. It was a mass of scars and raw patches that looked like meat.

"I'm Julian Quist. I wanted to talk with you if it's not too inconvenient."

"What are you, a reporter?"

"I'm a public relations man," Quist said, "at the moment trying to do a job for the producer of the show your ex-wife is starring in."

The man gave his wheelchair a quick jerk to one side so that his horror of a face was almost obscured. "I can't imagine how I could be any use to you," Bud Tyler said. "So, if you'll pardon me—"

"Sharon is making a lot of trouble for a lot of people," Quist said. "I thought you might help me find a way to make her see sense."

"Look, Mr. Quist, you obviously know I was once married to Sharon. If I knew how to get her to make sense, I might still be married to her."

"But I understand that you are still close," Quist said,

18

"and that she's helping you out with your troubles, medical bills and the like."

"If that is or isn't so it's none of your business, Mr. Quist."

"Of course it isn't, and it was a clumsy thing for me to say. I apologize."

"Who told you Sharon was helping me out with money problems?" Tyler asked, his voice harsh.

"Ian Moss, an actor friend of Sharon's. I needed sympathetic help. Moss thought you might be willing to give it."

Tyler's manner seemed to relax. "Nice old guy," he said. "Sharon used to think of him as a sort of surrogate father. He helped her get launched in her first film, years ago."

"Does she have family?" Quist asked. "Perhaps that's where I should go, not here."

"No family," Tyler said. "Her mother died of cancer when she was a small kid. Her old man drank himself to death after that."

"So there is a history of alcoholism?"

Tyler turned his tragic face toward Quist. "Are you saying that Sharon is drinking? She has a hatful of faults, Mr. Quist, but liquor has never been one of them."

"Something new, then," Quist said.

Tyler wheeled his chair into the room. His hostile attitude seemed to change. "Let's start over again, Mr. Quist," he said. "Tell me what your problem is. Sit down, if you like."

Quist sat in a comfortable overstuffed armchair. "Max Marsden, who is producing *Queen Bee,* is an old and very close friend of mine. He and his friends have invested several million dollars in the show. Sharon is driving them up the wall. She doesn't turn up for rehearsals, doesn't perform half the time when she does, often drunk they say. Not only are Max and his backers teetering on the edge of a

19

cliff, but scores of other people have jobs at stake—actors, stagehands, musicians, the director, set designer, choreographer, and on and on. Sharon's signed to a fabulous contract—twenty-five thousand dollars a week, plus ten percent of the gross, plus five percent of the profits, and she isn't pulling her weight."

"Not like her," Tyler said. His frown turned his scarred face into an ugly grimace. "She can be difficult, but she's a professional."

"That's what everyone thought. Of course, she hasn't done a stage play before."

"That's nonsense," Tyler said. "In her early days she did dozens of stage plays—summer stock, community theaters, road companies. Not Broadway, but working onstage is nothing new to her. She knows when she's ready, Mr. Quist. When there start to be paying customers she'll light up the sky."

"I hope you're right," Quist said. "Meanwhile, they don't know whether to risk it or not."

Tyler lifted his hands to his face. They were terribly scarred, too. "Do they have a choice?" he asked. "The production money is spent. She'll come through, you'll see."

"Could she be involved in some kind of unhappy love affair?" Quist suggested.

Tyler's laugh was bitter. "You asked if she was an alcoholic," he said. "She isn't. What she is . . . is a sexaholic! It's like an addiction over which she has no control. We . . . we were in love when we married—I thought. But she couldn't resist going after any attractive man who crossed her path. And what man can resist her when she makes it so openly possible? But grieving over someone she didn't get? Never. There's always someone equally attractive just around the corner, up a flight of stairs, 'across a crowded room.'"

"Must have been pretty tough for a young husband," Quist said.

Tyler touched his butchered face with the tips of his fingers. "I beat on her the first time I caught her out," he said. "And then—when I realized there was no way to stop her, no way she could stop herself—I divorced her. Then I began running risks I shouldn't have run. You see, in spite of everything, I loved her. I couldn't stand not to have her as my exclusive property, and yet I couldn't bear to be without her."

"And yet, when you smashed up, she came up with help for you?"

"I was making big money driving when Sharon and I first got together, married. She had a film she wanted to make—an independent production over which she'd have full control. I invested fifty Gs in the pre-production costs. The film was never made, but she still owns the property and still intends to make it some day. When I cracked up, she came to see me in the hospital. The plastic surgeons were trying to do something for me, and the costs were out of this world. Sharon offered to buy back my share in that unproduced picture. She knew that, in a way, she was responsible for what had happened to me. The plastic surgeons got most of the dough and left me like this." He clawed at his face. "There's nothing to grow anything on!"

"Rough," Quist said. He was silent for a moment. "I'm having her for dinner tonight. Can you suggest the best way for me to get her to tell me what's wrong?"

The words came from Tyler so bitterly it hurt to hear them. "Ask her in bed," he said.

Quist smiled. "As I told Ian Moss, I am 'otherwise engaged,'" he said.

"Our Sharon will be disappointed."

"One more question, if you don't mind," Quist said. "You say Sharon isn't a drinker. Hollywood is drowning in drugs these days. Could what someone thought was a drunken daze have been a drug problem?"

Tyler turned his wheelchair away again. "In all the time I

knew Sharon and lived with her she never drank. Oh, maybe a glass of white wine at some social gathering so she wouldn't look different. She saw her father go down the drain. She was afraid she might have inherited his weakness."

"Drugs?" Quist persisted.

"Not in my time, and it's out of character," Tyler said. "Let me make a guess for you, Mr. Quist. Sharon's sexual appetites make her very concerned about her appearance, her physical condition. She wants to look as perfect as—as she is. My guess is that she would never take anything, do anything, that would make her less than the most attractive and desirable woman in the world." That bitter little smile. "And she is that, you know."

"Thanks for giving me your time," Quist said.

"It was less difficult than I thought it would be," Tyler said.

"Can I come back some time and we can just talk about anything—the world in general?"

"Why should you?"

"Because you're a nice guy," Quist said, "and nice guys are not a dime a dozen."

A nerve twitched under Tyler's raw face. "If it would give you any pleasure at all it would be a ball for me."

2 Lydia Morton was in the kitchen of their Beekman Place duplex when Quist got home a few minutes past six. She was wearing a wine-red housecoat which Quist knew she knew was one of his favorites, protected by an apron as she worked at what she was preparing. She didn't turn to greet him.

"I bought fresh lobster—which I hope you can afford," she said. "It will make a nice Newburg which won't have to be cooked if your date is late getting here."

Quist heard the slight edge to her voice. "Half my date," he said.

"Am I expected to join you and the lady?" Lydia asked. "I thought you might be expecting me to put on my maid's costume and serve you. The lady won't like sharing you."

Quist reached out, took her arm, and pulled her, rather roughly, to him. "You damned idiot," he said.

She relaxed as he held her close. "I didn't know I could be jealous," she said.

"Double-damned idiot," he said.

"She *is* the most provocatively desirable woman there is, according to all the stories about her."

"That's because you've kept your light under a bushel," Quist said.

She smiled for the first time. "You've just got time to freshen up and put on your best bib and tucker," she said.

23

He walked over to a small service bar in the corner of the kitchen, pouring himself a Jack Daniels on the rocks, and sat down on the bar stool, "I'm not sure just how to make this work," he said. "I've just come from visiting with her most recent husband." He told her about the time spent with the dreadfully mutilated Bud Tyler. "She doesn't drink, Tyler says, which makes the story of her being drunk at rehearsals puzzling. He's certain she wouldn't be involved with drugs. It would be out of character for her to jeopardize so many jobs, just for some kind of temperamental whim. And yet something just like all those things is happening."

Lydia went back to the supper dish she was preparing. "You're so very male, Julian," she said.

"I'm glad you think so, luv."

"I didn't mean it as a compliment," Lydia said. "How male of you to think it was."

"So the music goes round and round—" Quist said.

"I simply meant to point out how chauvinistic it is for you to go around asking other men how to deal with a woman. This particular woman has had five husbands and God knows how many lovers who haven't known how to deal with her. It wouldn't occur to you to ask a woman, would it?"

He grinned at her. "I'm asking," he said.

She turned from behind the kitchen counter to face him. "I did some research on Miss Sharon Ladd—after you called to tell me I was expected to cook a dinner for her."

Quist's grin widened. "I called to tell you I expected you to protect me."

"I'm sorry I've been acting like a jealous woman."

"I find it quite flattering," Quist said.

"Oh, you—you—!"

"Male man," Quist said, laughing now. "So you researched the lady."

"Let's begin with five husbands," Lydia said. "The first was twenty years ago; she was nineteen and already had three very good film roles to her credit. He was Jack Conroy, young actor, quite good then and much better today. Films, a long-running series on TV. From all accounts a very nice, gentle guy—married again now, with several kids. Ask him about Sharon now and he'll laugh, and tell you she was a youthful aberration."

"Not any problem to her today?"

"Unless she has some crazy notion of going back and playing the field all over again. Jack Conroy learned his lesson all too well. He would stop her at square one if she had anything as absurd as that on her mind."

"Move on, luv."

"After Sharon had been married to Jack Conroy for about a year, she was sent to Europe to make a film. She was a star now. There she met Raul Sanchez, a millionaire Spanish nobleman. Sanchez's family made their fortune selling munitions to the fascists, back in the days when General Franco, Mussolini, and Hitler were ruling the European roost. While she was making that film, Sharon had a scandalous and quite open affair with Raul Sanchez. Money, and Rolls-Royces, and fancy watering places in the south of France. When she got home from making the film, Jack Conroy demanded a divorce and got it. Whether the studios brought pressure on her I don't know, but in any case she hooked her nobleman and he became husband number two. They hadn't had time for a honeymoon before her name began to be linked with every big male star in Hollywood."

"Seems as though marriage automatically sets her off in another direction," Quist said.

"Like a soldier who wins a war and has to find new fields to conquer," Lydia said. "The Sanchez breakup provided the press with more fun and games. It seems the young man had neglected to get a properly legal divorce from some previous bride. So Sharon was off and running, without problems."

"And the Spanish guy didn't need any money from her. She must have been starting to be pretty damn rich on her own by then."

"She never married a poor man," Lydia said.

"You ought to have a look at Bud Tyler," Quist said. His face darkened. "But I wouldn't wish that on you, the poor devil."

"He wasn't poor when she hooked him," Lydia said. "But let's keep it in order. After Sanchez there was Billy Lockman, Texas oil millionaire."

"More money."

"After the young Jack Conroy, which may have been a real romance, it has always been money—husbands and lovers. It may go hand in hand with sexual prowess in her mind."

"Then you can see how safe you are, luv," Quist said, smiling.

"I don't think of you as exactly broke," Lydia said, "and I know how good you are—horizontally."

"Nicest words of the year." Quist sipped his drink. "What happened with the Texas oil man?"

"There was another film scheduled for production to be directed by the great Leon Zuckermann."

"Ah, yes—'Hollywood's royal couple,' they were called."

Lydia nodded. "Hollywood's greatest woman star by then, Hollywood's most important and powerful producer and director. They had Hollywood dizzy—until Sharon ran off with Bud Tyler, the race car driver."

"Wait a minute, luv. What happened to the Texas oil man?"

"You could hear his screams all the way to the North Pole," Lydia said. "I guess he really loved the lady. There

26

were some kind of technicalities that permitted a quick divorce. She was evidently so irresistible that guys like the Spanish noblemen and Billy Lockman didn't get their decks clear before they made a dive for her. But Billy wasn't a quitter. He tried a solo invasion of the Beverly Hills Shangri-La where Sharon and Zuckermann were living. He got himself chewed up by a guard dog and a couple of security men Zuckermann had patrolling the place. More scandal. Two weeks later he got himself involved in a barroom brawl somewhere in Texas. Someone had said nasty things about Sharon, according to the papers. He wound up dead on the barroom floor, a bullet hole in his head. They say Billy pulled his gun first."

"A film in itself," Quist said. "We live in a pretty damn peaceful world, luv."

"So we come to Act Five," Lydia said. "Up comes Bud Tyler, handsome, glamorous, daredevil race car driver—records in the Indianapolis 500, in Europe, everywhere that cars are raced. You can get rich in sports these days. Off she goes with Bud to some place where he's driving. Zuckermann didn't give up easily. He hired Karl Kramer, the famous palimony lawyer. He sued Sharon for a million bucks, claiming she had damaged his reputation, his career, and had threatened his future."

"He needed money?"

"He made a lot, but he spent it every day of his life," Lydia said. "The case was settled out of court, I don't know how. But rumor has it that it cost Sharon a pretty penny. Kramer doesn't lose cases he takes."

"So who came next?" Quist asked.

"Nothing special," Lydia said, giving an indifferent shrug. "Bud was off racing, she was off making films. I guess she just started to play the field. Two years of that and Bud got himself a quiet divorce. Then his tragedy."

"She didn't desert him when he was in trouble," Quist

27

said. He told Lydia how Sharon had bailed out Bud on his doctors' bills.

"So she gets a very small gold star on an otherwise empty sheet," Lydia said.

The house phone, on the wall by the bar where Quist was sitting rang. He answered. "Oh! Well—send the lady up." He put down the phone and glanced at his watch. "Twenty to seven. Our guest is early."

Lydia gave her man a tight little smile. "It shows how eager she is, Julian."

"Don't be bitchy, luv," Quist said.

It had been quite some time since Julian Quist had looked at a woman with anything but an artist's eye for beauty and charm. Lydia was responsible for that. She had provided him with everything he could want, and he was convinced that anything else that might look intriguing could only be anticlimax. But he will admit, if you ask him today, that Sharon Ladd stirred memories of a time when he'd been a hunter, playing the field. If he had encountered her back then, he would have instantly shifted into high gear.

Standing at the door of his apartment, he could feel the electricity, the excitement she generated automatically. The golden hair, worn shoulder length, was exquisite. It looked youthfully casual, and yet Quist knew it must take hours of care. The wide blue eyes had a kind of youthful innocence to them, and yet a wicked little smile seemed to tell you at once that those innocent blue eyes were a fake. Her simple print dress Quist knew only a very rich woman could have afforded—and the bracelets, earrings and rings she was wearing.

"Julian! I'm afraid I'm early," she said in a low, throaty voice. This wasn't the harsh voice he'd heard in her dressing room earlier on. This was the purring sound of the jungle cat on the prowl.

28

"Better early than never," Quist said. "Come in, Sharon."

She walked into the large living room, looking around. She moved, he thought, with the grace of a ballet dancer.

"What a lovely room," she said. "And a terrace outside overlooking the river! The scene is always changing for you!"

"We find it very satisfactory," he said.

She turned, sharply, to face him. "*We?*"

Lydia chose that moment to come out of the kitchen. For a moment the dark-redhead and the blonde faced each other. A beauty contest judge would, Quist thought, have some difficulty choosing between them. The scales tipped Lydia's way for Quist, because he knew her to be warm and compassionate, while Sharon appeared to be brittle with an overdeveloped ego.

Quist introduced them. "Lydia is the top writer and researcher in my firm," he told Sharon. "I thought she should be here when we talked about how to best promote you and *Queen Bee.*"

"I'm not sure I understand what there is to promote about me that hasn't been used, by Joe Philbin and all the gossip jerks in the United States," Sharon said. "*Queen Bee* is based on a best-selling novel. What more can you want?"

"Warm stuff, personal stuff," Quist said. "Would you like to sit out on the terrace, or I think you'll find that armchair comfortable?"

Sharon was still eyeing Lydia. "What kind of 'warm' and what kind of 'personal'?" she asked.

"Just as it comes in chatting with you," Quist said.

"If you'll tell me what you'd like to drink, Miss Ladd, I'll bring it to you," Lydia said.

"A working girl in my business doesn't drink, thank you," Sharon said.

"Well, I have a lobster Newburg about to go on the fire," Lydia said. "If you'll excuse me—?"

Sharon's face was set in a hard, forced smile. "I came early because I had to apologize for walking out on my date with you. Something far more important than the story of my life has come up. So, if you'll excuse me—"

"I'm sorry," Quist said. "I'll walk you back to your hotel."

"That won't be necessary, Julian. I hope you won't be angry with me." She turned toward the front door.

Lydia gave Quist a puzzled look and took off for the kitchen. At the front door Sharon turned and looked up at Quist. The blue eyes were bright with anger.

"You didn't tell me you had a live-in girl friend," she said. She spun around and headed for the elevators. She waited, back to him, until the elevator came. She walked in without ever turning to look at him, and disappeared.

Quist walked back into the apartment. Lydia was standing in the kitchen doorway.

"The lady doesn't leave any doubts about what her intentions were," she said.

Quist grinned at her. "Not honorable."

"She's extraordinarily beautiful," Lydia said. "The only place I've ever seen her before was on screen and I supposed some of it was makeup and camera work. But she's something!"

"I'm not going to be much help to Max if I can't get her to talk about what's eating her," Quist said.

"There is a way, Julian. Just follow her back to her hotel—"

Quist put his arm around her. "Any more of that and I'll have to wash out your mouth with soap," he said.

Hours later Quist and Lydia were sleeping peacefully in the king-sized bed in their second-floor bedroom when the bedside phone woke Quist. The illuminated clock face by the phone told him that it was four in the morning.

"Julian?" a man's harsh voice asked when he had answered. "Max here."

30

"For God's sake, Max, do you know what time of night it is?"

"The ball game is over," Max Marsden said. "Murder!"

Quist felt a cold chill run down his spine. She had walked home, decked out in her fur, her jewels. "Some street mugger. . . ?"

"Hold onto your hat," Max said. "Sharon left the Beaumont, where she is living, about six-thirty. Where she went we don't know."

"She came here!" Quist said. "She was to have supper with us but she changed her mind after she got here. Lydia was a surprise to her."

Lydia was sitting up, her hand on Quist's bare shoulder. "What is it, Julian?"

"Sharon," he said. "Max says she's been murdered!"

"You've got it wrong, pal," Max said. "Let me tell you. Sharon came back to the hotel about seven."

"That would be about right if she went there direct from here," Quist said.

"Who should she meet in the lobby of the hotel but one of her ex-husbands, Leon Zuckermann. They came face to face, got into some kind of argument—shouting at each other in front of a fascinated crowd of onlookers. Suddenly Sharon hit Zuckermann across the face with her handbag and headed for the elevator, which took her up to her room on the thirtieth floor. What she did when she got there we don't know, but about five hours later she took her handgun, which she's licensed to carry, went down to the twelfth floor where Zuckermann had a suite, got him to let her in, I guess, and shot him three times—twice in the chest and once right between his baby-brown eyes."

"My God!" Quist said.

"Then she went back to her room, took some sleeping pills, and that's where they found her, sound asleep."

"She was seen going to Zuckermann's suite?"

31

"I don't know for sure. But it was her gun, found there in her room, three shots fired from it. Police say ballistics proves it's open-and-shut. She's charged with first-degree murder, possession of drugs, God knows what else. So *Queen Bee* is a sinking wreck."

"And so is Sharon Ladd," Quist said. "What did you want me to do?"

"There's nothing you can do. I—I just thought you should know."

"You've seen her, talked to her?"

"No."

"Does she have a lawyer?"

"I don't know. My whole world is collapsing around me, Julian."

"Where are you?" Quist asked.

"My office at the Tempest, trying to think up a funeral oration. For *Queen Bee,* not Zuckermann, who probably got what was coming to him!"

"Where are they holding Sharon?"

"Police—somewhere," Max said.

"I'll be in touch," Quist said.

3 When Quist switched on the bedside radio the story was there. A glamorous Hollywood star, at the apex of a brilliant career, had quarreled publicly with a ex-husband, and hours later—under the influence of drugs, it was suggested—had shot him to death in his hotel suite. And with this was a rehash of other marriages, other lovers, other scandals. There was one piece of information that was important to Quist. A brief statement saying that Sharon Ladd had been arrested and charged with Murder One plus possession of drugs, was issued by Lieutenant Mark Kreevich of Manhattan Homicide. Mark Kreevich was an old and close friend of Quist's. He was a new breed of cop, with a law degree, a taste for the arts, and an obsession with the idea that his world was fashioned upside down. Cops should be preventing crime and not solving them after they're committed. New York, his bailiwick, was a world center for crime and Kreevich spent a lot of his time trying to stay ahead of an invasion by criminals from all over the world. Solving a murder would not be Kreevich's dream of what he should be doing. But this one sounded easy.

Quist, when he had dressed and had a mug of coffee which Lydia had made while he showered and shaved, tried reaching Kreevich on the phone. The detective's home phone didn't answer, and police headquarters simply reported that the lieutenant was out on a job. He might still be, Quist thought, at the Beaumont, where the crime had been committed. After some delay the switchboard at the hotel located him.

"You must be psychic, Julian," Kreevich said. "I was about to try to call you. Thought I'd give you a little more time for sleep. It's just a matter of loose ends the District Attorney will want cleaned up."

"Loose ends?"

"Sharon Ladd says she spent an early part of the evening with you."

"About six-forty till six forty-five," Quist said. "Why is that important?"

"Her state of mind," Kreevich said. "Mainly, did you have any notion that she was speeded up on drugs?"

"No."

"Well, there was time for her to get bombed before she decided to go down to his suite and let him have it. She's still pretty far gone. Doctor says it will be a few hours before she can make perfect sense."

"Mark, has she confessed?"

"Who confesses?" Kreevich said, a bitter edge to his voice. "But this one's clear as a bell, Julian. Her gun, found in her room; ballistics proves it out. A few hours before, she'd had a big public row with Zuckermann in the lobby. Drugs found in her room. She got herself steamed up and decided to finish him off."

"But she says she didn't?"

"Wouldn't you, if it was the end of your life? You know the lady well?"

"Just met her yesterday morning," Quist said. "Invited her to supper. I was trying to help Max Marsden with the show she's starring in."

"Help him with what?"

Quist hesitated. "She's been behaving rather pecu-

34

liarly—missing rehearsals, drunk they thought, not performing. Max thought I might be able to find out what her trouble was. That's why I invited her over here."

"Did you find out—in a few minutes?"

"No. She said she had another date that was more important."

"So that's that," Kreevich said. "Well, thanks for telling me—"

"Hold it a minute, Mark. Could I come over there to the Beaumont and talk to you?"

"What's to talk?"

"I don't know for sure, Mark. I have an uneasy feeling about this. There are odds and ends that you might find useful."

"Julian, I've told you, this is open-and-shut, black-and-white. I'm just trying to make a complete case for the D.A.—while the stove is still hot."

"Maybe I could help."

"So, come ahead. You'll find me in Room Twelve-eleven, next door to where it happened."

"Be there in ten minutes," Quist said. "Will I be allowed to talk to Sharon?"

"Later in the day. She's in the emergency hospital here right now—still doped up."

"But the police have talked to her while she's in that condition?"

"Julian, we have a job to do, you know?"

Quist put down the phone.

"What *is* bothering you, Julian?" Lydia asked.

He touched her cheek with his fingers. "I don't really know, luv. An itch that I need to scratch, is the closest I can come to it."

The Beaumont was a familiar place to Quist. He often went there with Lydia at the end of a day at the office, had drinks in the famous Trapeze Bar, sometimes in the evening to the Blue Lagoon, a night club where there was always first-class entertainment. Sometimes they had dinner in the Grill or the main dining room. The hotel was like a small city within a city—restaurants, bars, shops in the lobby arcade, a bank, a hospital unit, a health club, and on and on. It had its own police force, maintenance crews, and hundreds of service employees.

At five-thirty in the morning the summer dawn was already spreading over the city. The city is different if that isn't your active time of day; fewer cruising taxis, more trucks and fewer private cars, almost no people on the sidewalks. As Quist walked the few short blocks from his apartment to the Beaumont he realized that, ironically, life moved on as usual in spite of what had happened only a few hours ago. Truck and taxi drivers probably knew about it from their radios, but it didn't stir emotions, just another headline. A man had been shot by his ex-wife, once removed, and a mentally disturbed woman was under arrest, facing God knows what, trying to pull herself out of a drug fog, but it was just a headline to millions of people. But somewhere, not here on the streets, there were people who cared or would feel the impact of what had happened. At the Tempest Theater Max Marsden was sweating out the problem of recuperating from a multimillion-dollar loss. *Queen Bee* was dead without its star, as dead as Leon Zuckermann in the police morgue. Scores of people involved in the production had dreamed of a long run and steady paychecks. This morning they had to think of new jobs somewhere else, not readily come by. Was there anyone who really cared what this would mean to Sharon Ladd? Was there someone to whom this meant more than the loss of a ticket to a profitable future? Her love life had made headlines for almost two decades, but was there someone somewhere who really loved her? Would Bud Tyler be grieving for her, or was he in a panic, knowing that a source of help in dealing with his shattered life might have suddenly come to an end? Hollywood moguls might be shocked by the unexpected loss of a million-dollar property, but was there one of them who might care about the woman herself?

Not too many people would be likely to grieve for Leon Zuckermann, Quist thought. This flamboyant and arrogant man had developed his success and his power in the film industry into a fine art for making enemies. The people who had used his talents, his near genius as a producer-director, to amass fortunes of their own might be shocked, but would they grieve? Not likely. All across the entertainment world the cliché would be "he got what was coming to him!" But somewhere, in some far corner, there must be someone who cared. Or was there?

As he approached the elegant entrance to the Beaumont, Quist asked himself why he was involving himself. Zuckermann was a zero to him. He had known Sharon Ladd for less than twenty-four hours, had no real knowledge of her except her sensual appetites, no tie to her that obligated him to help her. That was, however, his impulse that morning. It was a little like being a witness to a hit-and-run accident. You don't refuse help even though the victims are total strangers.

The Beaumont, at five-thirty in the morning, would have been strange to Quist at best. The cleanup crews would be mopping up after the night's traffic in the bars and night clubs, people you wouldn't ordinarily see in your normal comings and goings. Today was out of the ordinary for the regulars at that time of day. The lobby was crowded with people from the media, press, television and radio, all waiting for a glimpse of a glamorous killer. There were uniformed police, guarding the elevators and stairwells so that no one could drift into the upper regions where Sharon Ladd might be found or Lieutenant Kreevich interviewed.

Quist stood just inside the entrance looking around.

Some of the faces were familiar from other encounters with the newshawks. God, he thought, they were like scavengers! A hand rested on his arm, and he turned quickly, to find himself facing Mike Maggio, the night bell captain in the hotel who was an old acquaintance. Maggio, a dark-haired, bright-eyed veteran of the hotel's staff, who had grown up a smart street kid and was well equipped to deal with crises.

"Had an eye out for you, Mr. Quist. Lieutenant Kreevich told me you were on your way. You'll need help to get up to the twelfth floor, with all these goons ready to hang onto your coattails."

"How are you, Mike?" Quist said. "They do flock to the scene of the crime, don't they?"

Mike grinned. "'Frankie and Johnny were lovers,'" Quist said. "You see what happened when she got back here?"

"Just ease along with me," Mike said, disregarding the question. "I've got The Man's private elevator waiting for you."

"The Man," Quist knew, was a title given to the Beaumont's legendary manager Pierre Chambrun, who lived in a penthouse on the roof.

"Chambrun must not be pleased with all this," Quist said.

Maggio chuckled. "He says if the lady wanted to practice pistol shooting he could give her a list of possible targets that would have pleased him more."

They were edging through the crowd of press people toward the south bank of elevators. "What did happen here in the lobby, Mike?"

"Zuckermann was just checking in," Maggio said. "He'd flown in from the Coast and we'd sent one of our limousines to Kennedy to bring him here. I was handling his luggage instead of one of the regular bellhops. He has a reputation here for giving everybody a hard time." He laughed. "I'm

38

supposed to be able to take it better than most. Did you know him, Mr. Quist?"

"No."

"An overstuffed bantam rooster—or should I say pouter pigeon?" A little twitch at the corner of Maggio's mouth suggested distaste, "Everyone who had to do anything for him was dirt." The twitch spread to a grin. "I have to tell you I enjoy using the past tense about him."

"You got an alibi for the time he was shot?" Quist asked, smiling.

Maggio gave him a dead serious look. "Do you know, I asked myself that when I heard he'd been shot?" Then he laughed. "I had something of a run-in with him after the big scene in the lobby."

"Run-in?"

"You ever see him? Short, stocky, thirty pounds over-weight, cigar in the corner of his mouth, he was meaner than a hungry cat. He went to the desk to register. Atter-bury, the night clerk, had a suite held for him on the twenty-fifth floor, west side of the building. That wouldn't do! He had to have something that looked out on the river—the east side. We don't have empty rooms in this hotel, you know. Atterbury didn't have anything else to give him. I thought Atterbury was going to melt away under the desk, Zuckermann shouting at him, demanding to talk to The Man. Then somebody remembered we were holding a suite on the twelfth floor east for someone who was coming in later in the evening. Atterbury decided to take a chance that the later guest wouldn't gun him down if the reservations were changed and told me to take Zucker-mann up to twelve-oh-nine. Zuckermann was proud as a new bridegroom. He'd won a war. He promised Atterbury he'd complain to the boss about the clumsy way he'd been treated, warned me not to handle his bag as though it was a sack of potatoes, and we turned away from the desk."

"Sounds like a real charmer," Quist said.

"That was just the beginning," Maggio said. "There were a lot of people in the lobby, enjoying the row. What they were really waiting for happened just then. Sharon Ladd came in the front entrance. Ever since she's been staying here there've been people hanging around who aren't ordinarily here, waiting to get a look at her, ask for an autograph, snatch at her clothes. We have to help her get to the elevators."

"Why would she stay in a place like this where privacy would be impossible?" Quist asked.

"I think maybe she likes being the center of attention," Maggio said. "But, for sure, she didn't want attention from her ex-husband, and she almost ran him down before she realized he was there. He seemed to be enjoying himself.

"'Fancy meeting you here,' he said.

"She just stopped, staring at him. I don't think I ever saw a face so twisted with anger.

"'You bastard!' she said.

"He laughed at her. 'I hear you've been being a bad girl,' he said, 'driving old Max Marsden off his rocker. If he had known you as well as I do he'd have run a mile before he hired you to be in his opera.'

"She tried to walk past him but he blocked her way. 'I'm looking forward to being at your opening night,' he said. 'I'll get a kick out of watching you fall on your once-lovely face.'

"She was carrying one of those shoulder bags, leather, brass-studded," Maggio said.

"I know. I saw it."

"She took it off her shoulder and swung it at him like an Olympic shot-putter." Maggio laughed again. "She caught him right alongside the jaw with it and knocked him right on his fat ass! She ran for the elevators with the crowd cheering." Maggio's face darkened. "I bent down to help him up. 'Keep your filthy hands off me!' he shouted, and he

40

kicked out at me and caught me right in the shin. I started to take a swing at him but I managed to control myself. The guest is always right. He managed to get up and we went to the elevators on the east side. In the car he said, 'That crazy bitch is going to wish she'd never been born!' I got him to his room. No tip. End of story." Maggio shook his head. "When the news came down that he was dead— before we knew she'd done it—I began to wonder who could provide me with an alibi. People in the lobby had to know I hadn't loved him."

"How did you get to know she'd done it?"

"The police. That Kreevich is a smart operator. He heard about the row in the lobby and they went up to her suite on the thirtieth floor to ask her about it. They found her doped up, found the gun. Two and two make four."

Mark Kreevich was in 1211, where he'd said he would be. With him were a couple of plainclothes men and a uniformed cop operating a stenotype machine.

"Trying to put it together for the District Attorney," Kreevich said when he'd greeted his friend. "This one'll make so much noise the D.A. will want every detail nailed down tight. We're just putting the pieces together."

"Do they fit?" Quist asked.

"They should all be this easy," Kreevich said. "The trouble with this one is that all the way 'round the world half the people will be hoping she is guilty, and the other half will be hoping she isn't. No one's going to be indifferent."

"Has she got a lawyer?" Quist asked.

"She hasn't been clear enough, apparently, to make up her mind," Kreevich said. "Half a dozen high-priced legal beagles have been trying to get to her to offer their services—for a modest fee, of course. I suppose when people

wake up and hear the news, some of the studios in Hollywood, and probably your friend Max Marsden, will find her
someone."

"For a kind of silly reason I'd like to help her," Quist
said.

" 'Silly' isn't usually what motivates you."

Quist's smile was on the sheepish side. "She came to my
place tonight thinking she had a date with me. She found
out that Lydia is in my life. She went away mad. Maybe the
swing she took at Zuckermann was meant as much for me
as it was for him. If she would see me and talk to me I could
at least get our lawyer Bob Jacquith to protect her from the
wolves in the early stages."

"We're just doing our job, Julian."

"Did you have a search warrant to look for that gun in her
room, Mark?"

"We didn't need a warrant. It was sitting there, right on
her bedside table."

"She let you into her room, the gun was there, and that
was that?"

"If you're going to be sticky about this, I'd better start
from the beginning," Kreevich said. "About one-thirty in
the morning someone reported to the front desk that they'd
heard gunshots on this floor—Twelve. They thought the
shots came from Twelve-oh-nine. Hotel security people
came up here, found the door to Zuckermann's suite open,
went in, and there he was, shot to death in the sitting room
of his suite."

"The person who phoned the alarm?"

"A hysterical-sounding woman, according to Atterbury,
the night clerk at the front desk. Hung up before he could
question her."

"Wouldn't the switchboard know where the call came
from? Had to be somewhere on this floor, if they heard the
shots."

42

"The switchboard says one of their operators took an outside call asking for the front desk. She had no reason to check out or listen in."

"And no one has come forward to say they warned the front desk about the shots?"

"No."

"Doesn't it strike you as odd that someone on this floor heard the shots and went outside the hotel to warn the front desk?"

"'Outside' doesn't mean outside the hotel," Kreevich said. "It simply means not a room phone. There's a pay phone on every floor of the hotel, and banks of them in the lobby, the bars, the restaurants."

"But you've questioned the guests on this floor who *could* have heard the shots?"

"Of course. No one who had a room on this floor will admit hearing anything or calling the front desk. Eleven men, eight women, all negative. It's an old story. People don't like to get involved."

"So, when they found Zuckermann, the hotel people called the police?"

"Naturally. I was assigned to it."

"You got here, heard the story about the row in the lobby, and went to question Sharon?"

"We would have talked to her anyway," Kreevich said. "They were once married—an obvious connection."

"So you went up to the thirtieth floor, she let you in, and there's the gun?"

"Not quite," Kreevich said. "Sharon Ladd didn't answer her phone, didn't respond to a knocking on her door. Elevator man had taken her up to Thirty after the row in the lobby. She hadn't gone out after that."

"How did you know?"

"Hell, Julian, that lady can't go two feet without being seen and recognized. The Marilyn Monroe of 1983. Hotel security got us a passkey and we went in. She was in bed, completely out. I thought at first it was booze, but there was no liquor anywhere. Then we saw the gun on her bedside table and a bottle of sleeping pills. Naturally, I looked at the gun. Three shots had been fired from it—recently."

"So you got her awake?"

"Yes, but she was groggy, dazed. Didn't seem to take it in when we told her why we were there. When we asked her about the gun, she said she always slept with it where she could reach it. In her world, with her kind of fame, she lived in fear that someone would break in, attack her."

"Not unreasonable."

"But Zuckermann was shot three times, and there were three shots fired from her gun. Later there was no doubt. Ballistics. That was the murder gun."

"But she denied it?"

"Hysterically."

Quist was silent for a moment. "You just said Sharon couldn't go two feet without being recognized, noticed. How did she get from the thirtieth floor down to here without being seen. One-thirty in the morning, the hotel is still very much alive."

Kreevich shrugged. "It couldn't happen but it did," he said.

"Elevator operator not wanting to get involved?"

"I don't think so. People who work for Pierre Chambrun here in the Beaumont are pretty generally to be trusted. But the fire stairs could be deserted. It is only a few yards from the fire stairs on this floor to the door of Zuckermann's suite. If no one was out in the hall she could have covered that distance without being seen or recognized."

"The sleeping pills?" Quist asked.

"Seconal, a standard prescription sleep aid," Kreevich said. "Sharon says she's taken them for years. They come in

44

pull-apart capsules. She'd pulled them apart, all right; filled them with some kind of extra powerful amphetamines."

"She admits that?"

"No, but the police lab makes it certain. She got high on them after the row in the lobby, high enough to decide to go down and polish off Zuckermann, went back upstairs, took some more and conked out."

"Where is she, Mark?"

"Right here in the hotel hospital. We're holding her here until she clears up enough for the D.A. to talk to her."

"Without a lawyer or a friend?"

"So far," Kreevich said.

"I'm a friend," Quist said. "I'd like to talk to her. And I'd like to get Bob Jacquith here to represent her."

"I guess she's entitled," Kreevich said.

Even in a hospital bed, wearing a hospital gown, her golden hair uncoiffed, Sharon Ladd was a very beautiful woman. A uniformed cop sitting on a chair in the corner was reading the *Daily News.* Dr. Partridge, the hotel physician, an older man, somewhat cantankerous in his manner, seemed glad to see Quist.

"Police have been pretty high-handed with her, according to my book," he said. "No lawyer. You're the first friend who's come forward. Famous woman like this, you'd think she'd have been mobbed with helpers."

"I suppose most of them don't know what's happened," Quist said. "Six o'clock in the morning."

"Hell, thousands of people know!" Dr. Partridge said.

"Is she able to talk?"

"Able if she's willing," the doctor said.

Quist walked over to the bed and stood looking down at her. Her bright blue eyes fixed on him and in that moment she didn't look at all dazed or groggy.

45

"You still want to know something human about me?" she asked, with a bitter twist to her mouth.

"I want to help, if I can," Quist said.

"Get that crazy detective to listen to me!"

"He's not crazy," Quist said. "I know him quite well."

"Is it—is it true that Leon is dead?"

"I'm afraid it is, and the police have a pretty solid circumstantial case against you, Sharon."

"That's insane! I—I hated the bastard, but why should I kill him? He's long out of my life."

"Your gun. You were high on drugs."

"I've never taken any drugs in my life—except some Seconal when I can't get to sleep." Again the twisted smile. "I don't sleep well alone."

"Seconal tablets that you'd doctored with something a lot stronger and more dangerous."

She pushed herself up on an elbow. "You're crazier than that detective!"

"Lab tests show you were on speed of some kind," Quist said. "Ballistics shows that it was your gun that killed Zuckermann."

"None of that is true! The police are trying to frame me! Why don't they find out who really did it?"

"They think they have, and the evidence is pretty solid, Sharon."

She dropped back onto the pillow. "You believe that?" Her voice was reduced to a whisper. "Is that why you're here—to get me to confess?"

"What do you have to confess?" Quist asked.

She was up on the elbow again. "*Nothing!* Absolutely *nothing!*"

"I'd like to have you tell me about the evening," Quist said. "But before you do, I'd like you to authorize me to call my lawyer to represent you—until you choose one of your own."

"What do I need a lawyer for?"

46

"My dear Sharon, you're going to need an army of lawyers before you're through with this—unless we get lucky."

"*We* get lucky?"

Quist hesitated. "I can't quite tell you why I resist buying the facts, Sharon. The D.A., the grand jury and a trial jury will take them hook, line and sinker. You were drugged, you don't remember what happened, but it was your gun and you'd just had a public fight with Zuckermann. God knows what they'll dig up about your past relationship with him—marriage, divorce, a property suit. Motive, weapon. Let me get Bob Jacquith, my lawyer, over here and then we'll talk."

"Oh my God!"

"If Jacquith doesn't satisfy you, you can get someone else. But meanwhile they won't be able to run over you without legal protection."

"I'm nothing to you," she said. "Why are you helping?"

He smiled at her. "Lady in distress," he said. "Knighthood is in flower."

She sounded, suddenly, like a little girl. "I'd be very grateful, Julian."

Bob Jacquith, who had handled all the legal problems for Julian Quist Associates for the last ten years and was a close friend, was wakened by Quist from a peaceful sleep, having heard nothing about the murder at the Beaumont. Criminal law wasn't Jacquith's specialty, but he had started his legal career as an assistant to a district attorney in a small New England town.

"When we see just how tough it is," he told Quist on the phone, "I'll know whether I feel competent to handle it."

"Guilty or innocent, she's entitled to the best help she can get," Quist said. "At least with you we'll know you're not out to skim the cream off her bank account."

"It could be tempting," Jacquith said, chuckling.

"Get over here, will you, Bob!"

47

"Half an hour," Jacquith said.

When Quist put down the phone in the outer office of the hotel's hospital complex he found himself facing a wiry, dark little man with the coldest gray eyes he could ever remember seeing. They were like two newly minted dimes.

"Mr. Quist? I'm Jerry Dodd, head of security for the Beaumont. My boss has asked me to give you any assistance I can."

"Pierre Chambrun?"

"What other boss is there here?" Dodd asked.

"Why would he think you could help me?"

Jerry Dodd's thin mouth tightened. "He's a hunch player. He isn't comfortable about the way things are going. That puts him on your team."

"How does he know I'm not comfortable?"

"Let me tell you something for starters, Mr. Quist. The Man knows everything that goes on in his hotel, including what the third assistant dishwasher is thinking. I suspect Kreevich told him you were uneasy. That made two of you."

"What bothers him?" Quist asked.

"Madam X, who reported hearing shots on the twelfth floor," Dodd said.

"I understand they haven't identified her yet."

"That's why I call her Madam X," Dodd said. "Here's what's bothering my boss. Every room in this hotel is soundproofed. You could fire a cannon off in one of them and nobody in the next room, or in the hall, or *anywhere*, would hear it."

"Not if the door to the room was open, and if the killer went to the door, Zuckermann opened it and was shot."

"Zuckermann was found inside his suite, fifteen yards from the door."

"He could have been shot in the open door, staggered back into the suite," Quist said.

48

"One of those shots got him right between the eyes. He didn't stagger anywhere, dropped in his tracks."

"So the killer went to the door, Zuckermann opened it, the killer followed him into the suite, leaving the door open, and shot him."

Dodd's smile was grim. "Keep trying," he said. "If the door was left open, the shots would have been heard in the hall. Almost across from Twelve-oh-nine is the housekeeper's room. There are two night maids on duty there. They should have heard the shots. They didn't."

"They were in their quarters, door closed, and *their* room is soundproofed."

"Only guest rooms are soundproofed," Dodd said. "When this Madam X telephoned the desk to say she'd heard shots, we called the housekeeper's room on Twelve. The maids were on the job and they hadn't heard anything. We went up, began checking each room and suite. Guests in the first two rooms we checked hadn't heard anything. Twelve-oh-nine was closed and locked and nobody answered. I used a passkey to let myself in and found Zuckermann, well inside the suite, dead. The killer closed the door when he—or she—left. It locks automatically. My boss thinks it's possible Madam X knew what had happened, knew when the coast was clear, and then sounded the alarm. The medical examiner's boys can't tell within a half hour how long Zuckermann had been dead when we found him. What it boils down to, Quist, is that Chambrun doesn't believe Madam X heard shots from the hall, or in an adjoining room. He thinks she was in Twelve-oh-nine, did the shooting or watched it, and then sounded the alarm when she was safely away."

"Why sound the alarm at all? It would have been hours before you would have found Zuckermann normally—not until the maids came in the morning."

"It's guessing time," Dodd said.

"So guess."

49

Dodd shrugged. "Zuckermann was killed with Sharon Ladd's gun. That's not a guess. The gun was on the lady's bedside table when we went in there. She was drugged. But, in a way, she had sent for us. She could be Madam X."

"Why, for God's sake?"

"Her whole life had been involved with the art of calling attention to herself."

"But finger herself for a murder?"

"A way to get it over with fast. She knew they'd nail her sooner or later."

"Your Mr. Chambrun believes that?"

"No," Dodd said, his voice harsh. "That's why I'm here. I said maybe I could help you, but The Man thinks maybe you can help us—since you seem to be interested in helping Sharon Ladd."

"Lieutenant Kreevich knows all this?"

"Sure. He thinks we're dealing with such a complicated lady that the explanations for why she does anything will always be complicated. She was drugged, it was her gun, and that's enough for Kreevich—and any other sane man."

"You don't buy Chambrun's doubts, or mine?"

Dodd shrugged.

"Sharon's coming out of her fog about now," Quist said. "When I've had a chance to talk to her I'll get back to you. Tell your Mr. Chambrun I'm grateful for his doubts."

"He isn't trying to do you a favor," Dodd said. "He just doesn't want what he thinks may be a miscarriage of justice in his hotel. When Kreevich nails the lady to the barn door—and he will—The Man will be satisfied and won't give a damn whether you are or not."

"Until that happens I'll be able to talk to you or other hotel people?"

"Right now you're The Man's white-haired boy," Dodd said.

***

Dr. Partridge, the hotel physician, stopped Quist as he was about to reenter the room where Sharon Ladd was being held.

"Wanted to show you this," he said. "Might help you when you start to ask her questions." He held out an orange-colored capsule in the palm of his hand. "This is the kind of capsule that Seconal, a prescription sleeping drug, comes in. You can see, it pulls apart easily. But the capsules found in the bottle beside the lady's bed had been tampered with, Seconal discarded, and a powerful amphetamine put in its place."

"So she wanted something stronger," Quist said.

"Why go through the complicated process of emptying the capsules and refilling them?" Dr. Partridge asked. "If she wanted the drug and had it, she didn't have to go through that routine. She didn't have to hide it from anyone else."

"According to rumor, she didn't sleep alone often," Quist said.

"She wouldn't take sleeping pills if she was about to make love to someone, would she? I'm telling you, Quist, I think someone else played games with the woman's sleeping medicine. I've told my boss that, and I think he's told Lieutenant Kreevich that. Maybe Miss Ladd will give you some idea who might have had access to her medicine."

"So many places and people," Quist said. "Each time she got the prescription refilled—"

"You don't get a Seconal prescription refilled," Partridge said. "You can't just phone in for another dose. She'd have to get a new prescription each time from her doctor. Of course someone could have gotten Seconal prescribed for himself, done the doctoring somewhere else, and then switched bottles on Miss Ladd."

"Thanks for the lead," Quist said.

"Thank Mr. Chambrun," Partridge said. "He asked me to call this to your attention."

51

"It seems I have quite a lot to thank him for," Quist said.

"Understand, no matter how she got the stuff, it could account for erratic behavior. She could commit a murder and not remember it."

"Do you believe that?" Quist asked.

Dr. Partridge tossed the little orange capsule up in the air and caught it. "I don't know what I believe," he said. "It could be she was drugged and doesn't remember what happened. It could be she remembers perfectly well what happened and is playing games with us and the police. It could be that there is nothing for her to remember and that someone has framed her. You pays your money and you takes your choice." He tossed the capsule up again and caught it. "I wish you luck in trying to get her to come clean."

It appeared to Quist that Sharon was a little more alert when he went back into her hospital room and sat down on the chair beside her bed.

"You locate your lawyer friend?" she asked.

"Like most uncomplicated people, at six o'clock in the morning, he was at home, in bed, asleep. He's on his way."

She turned her head to look at the early morning sunshine at the window of the room. "Max Marsden seems to have deserted me. Somehow I wouldn't have expected that."

"His whole world is tumbling down around him," Quist said. "He did set me in motion."

"What's happened to his world?" she asked.

"His star is about to be arrested for murder. No show, huge investment lost, scores of people who counted on him—and you—out of work."

"You don't seriously think I'll be charged with murder?"

"All that's missing are the technicalities. They've given you time to recover from an overdose of amphetamines while they wrap up a nice, foolproof case against you. Your

52

next step after this room is jail, unless Bob Jacquith can come up with some way to stall them."

"But what kind of a case have they got against me?" she asked, her eyes wide.

"Your gun killed Zuckermann, to start with," Quist said.

She frowned. "I remember them saying something like that when they came to my room. I was groggy from the Seconal, still am. But of course it couldn't have been my gun. It was right there on my bedside table, where it always is."

"It was your gun, Sharon. No question about that. Ballistics."

"Ballistics?" She sounded vague.

"Science of identifying the gun a bullet was fired from," Quist said. "No two guns leave the same markings on a bullet. As individual and positive as fingerprints. Your gun killed Zuckermann. There's no question about that."

"But how. . . ?" Her voice trailed off.

"The police think it's simple," Quist said. "You had a public row with Zuckermann in the lobby when you came back here from my place. You went upstairs to your suite, loaded up on drugs, and some hours later went down to his room and let him have it."

"I don't take drugs!" she said. "Just the Seconal. I did take a couple, but they don't black you out. Just relax you and let you sleep. I never left my room. I never went anywhere near Leon or his room. I've never fired that gun in my life!"

"It was loaded, was fired," Quist said.

"No!"

"Tell me about the gun, why you have it, why it's on your bedside table when you turn in."

"I have the gun for protection. You don't know what it's like in my world, Julian."

"Tell me."

53

She took a deep, shuddering breath. "I have a house in Hollywood," she said, "but I don't spend very much time there. In today's film business you work in Europe, Africa, even China, and all kinds of strange cities and towns on location. I rarely sleep in my own bed, Julian."

Quist gave her a faint smile. "So I've heard," he said.

"Just that kind of gossip makes it dangerous for me," she said. "I stay in a motel somewhere when we're shooting on location, and some goon will break into my room and have at me! The gossip jerks have people believing I'd welcome any kind of male attack. Believe me, Julian, however much I may enjoy sex I want to make my own choices! And so I have a gun, I let it be known that I have a gun, and I'm ready to use it if I have to, but it's been enough just to show it. I've never had to fire it."

"You didn't feel safe here at the Beaumont? Maids on duty, a highly efficient security force?"

"And dozens of keys; passkeys, duplicate keys," she said. "Anyway, having the gun is a habit, has been for years. I just feel safer with it there, at the ready."

"And people know this?"

"There have been jokes about it, 'pistol-packing mama.' Unpleasant jokes, that I seduce men at gunpoint!" Her smile made her seem more alive. "I wasn't armed when I went to your apartment last night, Julian. I thought I was very polite when I saw your Miss Morton there to say 'no' for you. Oh, I was disappointed, Julian. I'd had you figured wrong."

"Let's stay with what's important," he said. "The 'Seconal' you took wasn't Seconal. They've had it analyzed. They know. Why would you bother to empty those capsules and put another drug in them?"

"That's absurd, Julian! My doctor in Hollywood prescribes it for me, the prescription is filled by a reputable pharmacist. I have to get a new prescription every time I run out."

"What you took last night was not Seconal," Quist said again. "It was a strong enough drug to send you off the rails."

"I tell you, they were my capsules, my prescription. I've never taken any other drugs in my life! Hollywood is snowed under with cocaine and other junk, but I've never even tried it for fun."

Quist was silent for a moment. He thought he knew the ring of truth when he heard it. Dr. Partridge's third guess began to seem like a real possibility. *It could be that there is nothing for her to remember and that someone has framed her.*

"Let's go somewhere else for a minute, Sharon," Quist said. "I told you that Max had hired me to hype up the promotion for *Queen Bee.* That wasn't entirely true. He was concerned about the way rehearsals were going. He said you didn't turn up sometimes without letting anyone know; that you were quite often drunk; that you—"

"I was never drunk! I don't drink!"

"Drugs, then?"

"No!" She twisted on the bed where she lay. "I've told you, never, not even to experiment, not even for fun!"

"Max said that sometimes you were magnificent, everything he'd dreamed of, and other times you just seemed to mumble your way through rehearsals."

"Max is full of it!"

"Joe Philbin, the PR man, told the same thing. I saw one of those mumbling moments yesterday before I came backstage to introduce myself."

She turned her face away from him. He could see that her whole body was shaking under the sheet that covered her. Her voice was unsteady when she spoke, her face still turned away.

"I have never been so scared in my whole life, Julian."

"Why not? Being accused of murder is a scary business."

"I'm not talking about that! I haven't murdered anyone.

55

Your lawyer will help me to prove that. It's what's been wrong with me—for the last three weeks!"

He waited for her to go on.

"I—I haven't done any theater for the last twelve or fourteen years," she said, her voice still unsteady. "All films. But I started out in theater and—and did summer stock, road companies, community theater. I—I understand the disciplines. When Max Marsden made this unbelievable offer for me to do *Queen Bee* I didn't have the slightest concern about handling it without any problems. It was a wonderful script, a fine director, an excellent cast. I couldn't have been happier, more excited, more ready. And then—then it happened."

Quist waited.

"The first few days of rehearsal went very well. One big, happy family. Everybody working well together, everybody dreaming of a certain hit. But that first week involved a lot of mechanics. I don't know if you know the story of the play—a woman from outer space comes to Earth and takes on a group of big-shot male crooks. I make my first entrance flying in from the balcony. Peter Pan stuff. This involves learning how to handle the machinery. It wasn't hard, but it took time to get it to work smoothly. Larry Shields didn't want to have to go back to it later, so we took about three days to get it down to perfection. It was tedious, but in that time we all got to know each other, developed the kind of confidence in every aspect of the operation that's necessary. Then we got to work, blocking the action on stage, and beginning to make it happen. I was on cloud nine. I knew I was going to make it big in my first starring role on Broadway." She raised her hand and covered her eyes with it. "Then it happened. I—I woke up one morning not feeling too hot. Tired, I thought. We'd been going at high speed for about a week. When we got to the theater, Shields decided to run through the last scene we'd rehearsed the day before in order to nail it down. I was in the wings, waiting for my cue—and suddenly I didn't know what the cue was, where I was supposed to go when I got it, what my first lines were! I drew a complete blank!" She lowered her hand from her face. "Nothing like that had ever happened to me before, not ever. I'd never forgotten a line in my life. I thought it could only be a matter of seconds. I stalled around, made a small scene about something—but it didn't come back. I said I was feeling sick, and asked for a few minutes' break. I got my script off in a corner, saw what I was supposed to do, went back on stage and walked through the scene, script in hand. Larry Shields was burning. He called off the rehearsal for the day and shouted at me to get hold of myself!" She laughed, a bitter laugh. "I came back here to the hotel. If I was a drinker I'd have gotten drunk. If I took drugs I'd have taken them. I have another addiction, as you may have heard. A nice young man who'd been on my trail for a while. We had a lovely afternoon—and evening—and night. And the next day it was as if nothing had happened at all. I was all there, knew every line cold, every movement exact. All was forgiven until two days later, when it happened all over again."

"Your young man wasn't available before that?"

Sharon shook her head.

"Did you go to a doctor?"

"Yes. I don't have a doctor here in New York, but I asked Tommy Thompson, the assistant stage manager, who'd been very nice to me, to recommend a doctor."

"And the doctor said—?"

"Fatigue, stress resulting from what had happened. He said temporary amnesia wasn't unusual in cases like that. He gave me something to help me relax."

"Did he tell you you could go on taking your sleeping pills?"

"Yes. He said what he gave me wouldn't clash with the Seconal."

"And did it work?"

"No. The same ghastly blackout the next day."

"And after that?"

She smiled at him. "You invited me to dinner. I thought you were going to be the medicine that would get me off the ground today. That didn't pan out. I came back here, had my run-in with Leon, went to my room, took my sleeping pills, and that was absolutely that. I never left my room, never went to Leon's room. I was asleep when the police came to question me."

You pays your money and you takes your choice, Dr. Partridge had said—a frame-up or a cover-up, with a brilliant actress making the cover-up seem believable. If that was it, she was going to have to give an Academy Award performance to get around the ballistics report and the lab analysis of the drug she'd been substituting for Seconal.

But frame-up?

"Sharon, you are either telling me the truth or you are acting your lovely head off," Quist said. "On the chance that you are telling me the truth—"

"Julian! Why in God's name would I lie to you?"

"To cover up the truth. But let's say you're telling me the truth—the truth as you know it. Then this is what you have to face. Someone had access to your sleeping pills and substituted a potent drug for what was in the capsules. That drug may have caused the 'temporary amnesia' that's been plaguing you."

"Why, Julian?"

"Someone hates you, wants to see you fail."

"Oh, my God!"

"That's not all, Sharon. Last night—if you're telling the truth—you took that potent drug, assuming it was Seconal, and bombed out. Then one of two things happened. You

58

took your gun, sleepwalked your way down to Zucker-mann's room unseen, shot him and sleepwalked back to your room and passed out. Or—"

"Or what, Julian?" She reached out a pleading hand to him.

"Or you took the pills you thought were Seconal and passed out. Then someone came into your room, took your gun, went down to the twelfth floor and shot Zuckermann, brought the gun back to your room on the thirtieth floor and replaced it on your bedside table, and then called the front desk to tell them shots had been heard on the twelfth floor."

"Why?"

"To frame you."

"No one could ever believe that script, Julian."

He took her cold, shaking hand in his and held it gently. "Just for now, Sharon, that's what I believe, until someone proves to me it isn't so."

PART TWO

1

Bob Jacquith, Quist's lawyer, was a slightly disheveled, owlish-looking young man, peering at the world through large horn-rimmed glasses. No one would spot him for a tough, rough-and-tumble fighter in any kind of legal wrangle. That deceptive appearance was one of his assets, perhaps carefully cultivated.

Jacquith arrived at the Beaumont exactly when he promised, and was introduced to his client. Sharon was persuaded to authorize him to act for her, and then he and Quist went down to the hotel's grillroom, where they discussed the situation over an early breakfast. Quist put it to Jacquith just about as he'd put it to Sharon—a frame or a cover-up.

"And you buy the frame?" Jacquith asked. He had poured himself coffee but he wasn't drinking it. His eyes were narrowed behind his large glasses.

"For now," Quist said. "Someone, including me, will have to prove it wrong."

"Kreevich won't buy it," the lawyer said. "Certainly the D.A. won't buy it."

"Kreevich will at least listen," Quist said. "He's an old friend and he knows I'm not a fiction writer."

"So convince me," Jacquith said.

63

Quist put it together, as much for himself as for the lawyer. Sharon's history suggested she could have a variety of enemies: rejected lovers, movie people jealous of her meteoric climb to the top in films, women who had lost their men, her ex-husbands who had been cut off from her financial success.

"You're talking about dozens of suspects," Jacquith said.

Quist gave him a sour smile. "Maybe hundreds," he said. "There are religious freaks all over the place who may think of Sharon Ladd as a symbol of sin. God knows she's had enough *Enquirer*-type publicity, rumors that she's been in the hay with every man she's ever seen with. Then there are just plain creeps, lusting for a famous target to make an impression on someone."

"So where the hell do you start looking?" Jacquith asked.

"We could get lucky," Quist said. "The person we're looking for has to have spent time recently here in the Beaumont—had to have access to Sharon's room and her sleeping pills, had to have been moving from the thirtieth floor with Sharon's gun to the twelfth floor, and then back up to Thirty to replace the gun. This hotel is full of sharp-eyed people, Mike Maggio, the night bell captain, for one. If the security people here know what we're looking for they just might come up with something."

"'Beautiful Dreamer,'" Jacquith said.

"It's our best chance. Spend some time with Sharon. Talk to her, see if she can come up with any suggestions. I'm going to talk to Dodd, the security man, and Mike Maggio, if he's still on duty. After that I'm headed for the Tempest. People in the *Queen Bee* company may come up with some kind of reasonable guesses."

"They're going to arrest this woman and take her to jail," Jacquith said. "I can't stop that."

"That's not the end of the world if we can get a lead to the real killer," Quist said.

Jacquith took off his glasses, blew on them, and wiped them with his handkerchief. "If you should be right about this, Julian, I think you should be warned. The creep you're looking for is a psychotic killer. Mess around with him and you could be his next target."

"Sharon is his target, whoever he is," Quist said.

"You make it clear you're trying to get her off the hook and you could be in big trouble," Jacquith said.

From a public phone in the Beaumont's lobby Quist called Lydia at the apartment and brought her up to date on what was cooking. He didn't mention Bob Jacquith's warning because, in fact, it hadn't begun to sink in yet. He had often made a joke about "famous last words—that kind of thing could never happen to *me!*" That was his subconscious reaction to Jacquith's suggestion that he might make himself too interesting to a killer.

"What can I do to help?" Lydia asked him.

"There is a vast written history of our Sharon over the last fifteen or more years," Quist said. "Gossip columns, news stories, feature articles, reviews of films. Buried in those bales of stuff may be the story of a quarrel, a threat; even lawsuits for damages, alienation of affections, that might involve someone who is on the scene here in New York today. Turn some people at the office loose on it. It could be a long chore that produces nothing, but—" and he laughed— "not boring! Sharon doesn't make boring copy."

"And you?"

"I'm on my way to the Tempest. There will be friends there, possibly enemies, certainly gossip, and a small army of people eager to prove Sharon's innocence. Their bread and butter may depend on it."

"Watch your step, my darling," Lydia said.

"Meaning?"

"You could be playing with a live bomb, Julian."

That brought him up short. The only two people who'd heard his theory, Lydia and Bob Jacquith, had had the same reaction. He could be in danger. So, Buster, just keep your eyes open!

As he left the phone booth, Quist saw Jerry Dodd across the lobby talking to the day bell captain who'd just come on duty. Johnny Thacker, blond, trim, shrewd-eyed, had been a "hello" acquaintance of Quist's from a hundred luncheons in the Beaumont. The two men listened to Quist's brief outline of what he had done.

"A couple of questions you could help me with," Quist said.

"Glad to help," Thacker said. "The lady's been here for about three weeks now. I could say she's a little too much on the caviar side to suit my New England palate, but she's never asked for unreasonable help, is generous with her tips, and she doesn't treat the help as though they were slave labor. I'd like to help her—although I don't see how she can beat the case the police have built."

"She can beat it if it isn't so," Quist said. "My first question for you is the obvious—access to her room. Someone got in there to doctor her sleeping pills, or replace them with a doctored bottle. That same person got in there when she was asleep, took her gun, used it, and then got back in there to replace it. That suggests a key."

"There are keys, of course," Johnny Thacker said. "The maids on that floor have keys. They go into the rooms when the guests are out, to make the beds, change the linens, vacuum and neaten up. Those keys are carefully kept and guarded by trusted people. I suppose someone *could* get one of them."

"A bribe?"

Jerry Dodd made an angry little gesture. "When the day comes that we can't trust our help, we're out of business," he said. "A bribe is way, way down the line, I think."

66

"There are extra keys at the front desk," Thacker said, "but they aren't handed out to just anyone who asks for them. They're very carefully guarded. They wouldn't give anyone a key without an okay from Miss Ladd. Guests, when they leave the hotel, are supposed to turn in their keys, but they don't always. I can check out at the desk and see what Miss Ladd's habit has been about leaving her key."

"Ten to one she doesn't leave it," Dodd said. "I was here last night when she had her row with Zuckermann in the lobby. She didn't stop at the desk for her key, just went on up to her room after she flattened Zuckermann. So she had the key then."

Johnny Thacker grinned. "Lot of male traffic up to Thirty in the last three weeks. Maybe the lady gave one of her boyfriends a key."

"Would someone know how many keys there are?" Quist asked.

"Yes," Thacker said. "I could check to find out if more than one, Miss Ladd's, is out of our possession."

"Do that, will you?" Quist turned to Jerry Dodd as Thacker took off. "Would you, or Thacker, or Mike Maggio, or any of your security people notice anyone who'd seemed to be particularly interested in Sharon's comings and goings since she's been here?"

"Look, Mr. Quist, in the course of a week three, four, five thousand people circulate in and out of this place—the guests, transients in restaurants, bars, the night club. We can't possibly concentrate on identifying every person we see. People who act suspiciously, or are drunk or drugged out we keep an eye on. As for people who are interested in Miss Ladd—she can't blink an eyelash that people aren't interested. You deal with famous people every day of your life, Mr. Quist, but if you were here in the lobby and Sharon Ladd walked through, you'd be interested! You'd watch, wouldn't you?"

67

Quist nodded.

"As to who actually visited her here in the hotel—the desk may have sent up a name for her approval now and then. Mostly people just use the house phones over there, call the person they want to see, and go up."

"No extra protection for a big star like Sharon?"

"Of course there is," Dodd said. He sounded impatient, like a parent explaining something to a backward child. "We make sure people don't just go and hang around in the hall outside her room. We urge her, if she doesn't want to go public, to go straight down to the garage in the basement where one of our limousines will take her where she wants to go. We make sure, if she goes into one of our bars or restaurants, that she isn't annoyed by rubberneckers. We try to keep the press away from her unless she lets us know that she wants to see them."

"What about her nighttime boyfriends that Thacker mentioned?"

Dodd shrugged. "If they came late, or left in the early hours of the morning some of our night crew might see them, even recognize them, be able to put a name to them. The lady doesn't carry on with nobodies, you know?"

"Could you get me a list of people who were recognized?"

"I can try. The night people are all gone by now. I might not have anything for you till tonight."

"Please do what you can," Quist said. "Unless I can come up with something pretty fast, Miss Ladd's going to be carted out of here and taken off to jail."

"She can raise bail, no matter how high it's set," Dodd said.

"If they allow her bail," Quist said. "Murder One?"

"You really think she's been framed, don't you?"

"I need to be convinced she wasn't," Quist said.

***

The Tempest Theater, normally deserted in the early hours of the morning, was a center of public curiosity when Quist arrived there just before eight o'clock. The press was there in force, and a modest crowd of just simple gawkers were on the sidewalk. The stage door alley was blocked by police, and Quist was stopped in the lobby by a uniformed cop. Word was finally sent up to Max Marsden, after some argument and identification routines, and Quist was let in to the dark theater. The only illumination came from a work light on the stage.

Marsden's office was on the floor above the theater auditorium and Quist found it after climbing a darkened stairway. Max was sitting at a large flat-topped desk facing a scattered stack of papers. Unshaven, he looked something like a living corpse.

"How is she?" he asked, not bothering with a greeting.

"Coming out of it," Quist said.

"Drugs?"

"Let me tell you, Max. She was drugged, but it was by sleeping pills that had been tampered with by someone. I believe she was knocked out through the whole thing, her gun taken, used, and returned."

Max sat up very straight in his chair. "You mean she didn't kill him?"

"That's what I believe, Max, but I've got to prove it. The police and the D.A. will probably bring charges against her."

Max slumped back in his chair. "So we lose," he said.

"It would be helpful if you cared a little more for her and a little less for yourself," Quist said sharply.

The old man gripped the arms of his chair. "I have to think about my friends who've invested in this, the people in the show—and myself," he said.

"You'd like to save it, wouldn't you?"

"How? We've sold the show with Sharon Ladd as the star. Without her we're just a punctured balloon."

69

"Keep the rehearsals going, the previews started. We may still get your star for you."

"You know that every day we keep on, more and more money goes down the drain. There are rehearsal salaries, crew costs, writers' royalties, utilities, theater rent, musicians, the works. Without Sharon we just can't make it."

"If there is any chance of getting her, would you go on?"

The old man looked at Quist with heavy-lidded, exhausted eyes. "Show me the chance," he said.

"Someone has been on her back from the very start," Quist said. "She's been drugged without her knowledge by someone who had access to her suite at the Beaumont. She thought she was suffering from some kind of temporary amnesia brought on by fatigue and stress. She tried to hide that from you by pretending to be a temperamental bitch. Now she's been framed for a murder by someone who's been watching her closely. If she hadn't had that public row with Zuckermann in the hotel last night, a row that was seen by this person who's been watching her, Zuckermann might be alive today. Someone saw something that could be taken as a motive and went to work. If I can prove that, Max, you'll still have a star."

Max was silent for a moment, and then he asked, "How can I help?"

"Keep the rehearsals going with the understudy. There is an understudy?"

Max nodded.

"Let me talk to Larry Shields and anyone else in the company who's close to Sharon."

The old man seemed to come a little bit alive. "Larry's here in the theater. I'll send for him. He's been sweating it out along with the rest of us." He picked up the phone, got someone, and asked for Shields to be sent up to the office. "The person who's closest to Sharon is probably Janet Lane. I don't know if she's here or not."

"Sharon's dresser?"

"She's quite a little more than just a dresser," Max said. "She's an old friend whose own career came to an end some years ago. Sharon's been helping her by giving her a job. I think they've known each other since Sharon's early days in films."

"She could be a gold mine," Quist said.

The very nature of Julian Quist's business made him at least a casual acquaintance of many people in show business. Larry Shields was a man he spoke to on the street, in the grillroom at The Players, Sardi's or some other gathering place for actors, writers, artists, musicians. They called each other by their first names, a show business habit, even though their contacts had been casual and impersonal.

Shields was a big, athletic-looking man of about forty, with dark hair and eyes; he stood an inch or so taller than Quist's six feet. He'd directed a half dozen Broadway hits, primarily musicals, was professionally respected, with a gift for handling conflicting personalities and melding them into a working, going concern.

"It seems we've got all hell to pay, Julian," he said as he walked into Max Marsden's office.

"Julian thinks it may not be as bad as we thought," Max said.

"I suppose we could find another star," Shields said. "But that would mean expensive delays. You can't just be a quick study and walk into this part overnight. The technical aspects, the flying sequences, have to be endlessly rehearsed to get them to work smoothly and effectively. Not that Sharon's been easy to work with! But at least she's been drilled in the difficult part of it."

"Julian thinks we may still have Sharon," Max said.

"And more cooperative and at her best," Quist said. He went on to explain his theory to Shields, to explain Sharon's blackouts in rehearsal which had thrown her into a panic

71

and made her behave as she had because she was afraid to admit that there was something wrong with her. "There's no question that her sleeping pills have been doctored, that she was being affected by a drug she didn't know she was taking."

"Damn! I should have been smart enough to recognize something like that," Shields said. "I thought she was boozing it up."

"I don't think so, not even when she was in a state of panic. She did talk to someone named Thompson who recommended a doctor to her."

"Tommy Thompson is our assistant stage manager," Shields said. "He's never worked for me before, but he seems like a highly competent operator. He—he tried his best to get Sharon onto an even keel."

"I'd like to talk to him, along with Janet Lane," Quist said.

"Janet's the closest to a personal friend Sharon has in the company," Shields said. "They were both up-and-coming young film actresses in Hollywood twenty years ago. Sharon skyrocketed. Janet blew it somehow. Films are not my thing, so I've only heard rumors. The story is that Janet was blacklisted in Hollywood about ten years ago, couldn't get work anywhere as an actress."

"Blacklisted?" Quist asked. "Political? What?"

Shields shrugged. "I don't know. It may not even be true, just gossip. But she didn't work. I understand Sharon took her on as a sort of secretary–maid–companion. An act of genuine friendship for which Sharon isn't famous."

"I understand she helped out her ex-husband, Bud Tyler, who had troubles," Quist said.

"It's kind of crazy," Max said, "but I have the notion that Sharon tried to hide any acts of kindness she let herself perform."

"The whole film industry would have been on her back if it was known she was a soft touch," Shields said. "I can understand her hiding good deeds. Her kind of fame puts you at the top of every sucker list."

"Had she selected a lover in the company?" Quist asked.

Shields laughed. "Interesting woman," he said. "Her way of life, her lifestyle you might call it, would be considered highly immoral by your churchgoers' rules. But Sharon has her own rules, which, so far as I know, she's broken only once. She never lets herself get involved with a man who's working with her on the particular project of the moment. She doesn't let herself get involved with her leading man, her director—no one in the company. It would get in the way of a good, professional job of work."

"Never?"

"Oh, I don't say that after a film is finished or the run of a play is over she doesn't let herself become involved with a man she's been working with. But not while the project is ongoing."

"One exception, you said."

Shields's face hardened. "Leon Zuckermann," he said. "Some payoff!"

"Tell me," Quist said.

"Well, look at the record—as someone used to say. Her first husband was Jack Conroy, an actor; but they never worked together. Number two was Raul Sanchez, a Spanish nobleman with no connection to show business. Number three was Billy Lockman, a Texas oil millionaire without any theater or movie ties. Number five was Bud Tyler, a race car driver. I suppose you could say race car driving is a kind of show business, but not her kind. But number four was Leon Zuckermann, show business from the soles of his feet to the top of his ugly head. Rumor has it that no actress could work for Leon without first spending some time on his casting couch."

"They say that about all big shots in my business," Max Marsden muttered.

"In Zuckermann's case it was true," Shields said. "Zuckermann was the Fellini, the Ingmar Bergman, of American films, a brilliant director, unbelievably sensitive and tasteful for a man who was, personally, such a jerk. When he hired Sharon to star in one of his productions, the gossips had a field day. It was assumed that Sharon was in the hay with him. But I happen to know it wasn't so."

"Oh?"

"Zuckermann's lawyer Nate Epstein is a guy I had dealings with, buying a property for the stage from one of his clients. Nate gave me the lowdown when he heard Sharon had been hired for *Queen Bee*." Shields shook his head as if he couldn't believe what he was about to report. "Zuckermann apparently made his usual pitch. He couldn't work with an actress until the sexual excitement between them had been settled. Sharon laughed at him, told him to go fly his kite somewhere else. I guess Zuckermann was really hung up on her. He wanted more than an afternoon on that famous couch. He proposed marriage, believe it or not. That's how much he wanted her. Nate says it was a very carefully worked-out business arrangement before she agreed. She was to star in his next three films. He was to pay her whether he used her or not. He was hungry enough to say yes. When the business aspects of it were all settled, they were married—big Hollywood wedding. And then she laughed at him once more and walked out on him! He never got what he'd given his right arm for."

"The lawyer knows that?"

"Sure. He represented Zuckermann in a suit to break the agreement. They lost the suit. Zuckermann had a star who had made him a laughingstock and taken him to the cleaners financially."

"But it's Zuckermann who's dead, not Sharon," Max Marsden said. "You can understand how he might want to hurt her, but not the other way around. She'd had it all her own way."

"That encounter in the Beaumont's lobby last night gave the killer something to work with, probably speeded up his plans," Quist said.

Shields's raised eyebrows showed his disbelief. "You're suggesting that Zuckermann really wasn't the killer's target? That he was just a pawn in a game in which the object was to capture the queen?"

"Someone's been maneuvering her into taking a fall ever since you went into rehearsal," Quist said. "The right moment came to lower the boom—and it was lowered."

"God knows, I hope you're right," Shields said. He took a deep breath and let it out in a long sigh. "I'd welcome her back in the show, as I'm sure Max would."

Max's smile was bitter. "All you stand to lose, Larry, is another feather in your cap. I can lose every red cent I've got, plus my friends' money, plus the trust and confidence of future investors."

"It's rough on you, Max," Shields said. "You break a lifetime rule, put your own money in a show, and you find out how right you'd always been—before that."

Max brought his fist down on the desk. "This was so sure-fire!"

"Don't give up, friend, just yet," Quist said.

At that moment Janet Lane burst into Marsden's office. From his brief encounter with her the day before Quist had thought of her as a plain, almost dowdy-looking middle-aged woman. Now that she was animated, wide-eyed, he could see the remnants of what must have been a very handsome young woman—high cheekbones, bright eyes, a wide, generous mouth.

"It's not true, is it?" she asked in a shrill voice. "She didn't kill him, did she?"

"The police think she did," Shields said. "Quist has some doubts."

"We met yesterday, Miss Lane," Quist said.

75

"My God, I was just getting my breakfast," Janet Lane said. "I switched on the radio and there it was!"

Max Marsden got up from his desk, moving like a man whose every bone ached with fatigue. "Larry and I have got to go down and talk to the company."

"Closing?" Janet asked.

"Not just yet," Max said. "Quist has convinced me we should hang on for a little longer. There's just a chance. . ."

"I'd appreciate it if you'd stay and talk to me for a few minutes, Miss Lane," Quist said.

The woman sank down in an armchair by Marsden's desk and covered her face with shaking hands. Marsden and Shields left the office on the way to talk to the assembling company. Quist waited for a moment or two while the woman obviously fought for self-control. Then, in a very quiet voice, he began to outline the facts he had, the doubts those facts had created.

"I understand you and Sharon have been very close for a long time, Miss Lane. You could help," Quist said.

Janet Lane lowered her hands. Her lips were trembling. "Anything," she said. "Do you know something, Mr. Quist? I have a lot more reason for wishing Leon Zuckermann dead than Sharon had."

Quist waited for her to go on. Time was vital, but hurrying this woman just now could shut off important information.

"Sharon and I started out in films at about the same time," Janet said, "more than twenty years ago. She was so damn beautiful she didn't need any credentials. Can you believe I was Miss Utah, and a runner-up in the Miss America contest?"

"I believe," Quist said. "I have a hunch you're playing the role of Sharon's dresser and companion. I have a feeling that if you wanted to you could light up the sky a little again."

76

"It's a way to keep people from pitying me," she said.

"Why should they pity you?"

"Because I could have been up the ladder, maybe not as far as Sharon, but somewhere up there—if it hadn't been for Leon Zuckermann."

"Want to tell me?"

She nodded. "I—I crossed Zuckermann's path long before he ever knew Sharon. I—I was subjected to the Zuckermann treatment. If I would have sex with him, I could have a part in one of his masterpieces. I don't know, Mr. Quist, but I guess I thought that was the way you got anywhere in Hollywood, that that's how Sharon was getting where she was getting. Anyway, I—I let Zuckermann have his way with me, and I got the part I wanted. It was a loathsome business; he is—was—a loathsome man. In the end I couldn't go on with it, not even if he could make me a star—something I wanted more than anything else in the world. But I couldn't stand him, and so I told him 'No more!' I knew I wouldn't ever work for him again. What I didn't know was that I wouldn't ever work anywhere again in films. They'll deny it in Hollywood, but there is a blacklist, and Zuckermann had the pull, the power, to put me on it. I was done as an actress."

"No work at all?"

"Not in films or television. I got some work in radio, using a phony name. None of what Sharon calls the Hollywood Mafia could see me working on radio. I was just Jane Lewis, a voice. Sharon tried to get me a part in one of her films, a walk-on, but the minute I showed up on the set I got the gate!"

"Sharon didn't have the drag to override that?"

"She tried. No, she didn't have that kind of drag."

"The blacklist really works, then?"

"Oh boy, does it work! I had no living family, no one to turn to. I hadn't any training in any other skills. I thought that sooner or later the big boys would forget about me. I wasn't that important. But I was wrong. They're like the elephant who never forgets. Sharon, headed for the very top of the mountain, didn't forget me. She took me in to live with her. She still had the little cottage in Beverly Hills where she and her first husband, Jack Conroy, had lived. Nothing grand. She was never at home enough to have a grand place—making films in Europe, in Asia, and on location all over the country."

"It must have been difficult sharing a place with her with all the men in her life," Quist said.

"Not really. That cottage, for Sharon, was a refuge from the rest of her life. She didn't bring her men there. I stayed there when she was away, no rent to pay, charging groceries to her accounts. It was friendship, and—and it was charity. She sensed I wasn't comfortable that way, and so she offered me a job. It was real enough, she needed the help. I was a secretary, answering fan mail and other stuff; I was her what-you-might-call wardrobe mistress. It would just be a stopgap until the ice broke for me. It never did. It's been years now, Mr. Quist. In that time Sharon went off to Europe and married her Spanish nobleman. Later on, she went on location in Texas and married her oil millionaire. Then, much later, she came home to the cottage one night and told me she'd had a call from Leon Zuckermann to star in one of his epics. I told her what she'd have to pay for it, and she just laughed at me. 'I'll fix that bastard's wagon as a special birthday present for you,' she told me. She played him like a trout on a hook, giving nothing until he was prepared to give everything. There was the marriage and then the final bucket of cold water in his face. He never got even the smallest taste of what he was after. Divorced again, and lawsuits and Zuckermann, because of a premarital contract, had to pay her for three films she never made—millions of dollars. Most of this was to get even for *me!* Can you imagine?"

"By then she did have the power."

"But not to get me off the blacklist. Zuckermann knew why she'd treated him as she did, and if I ever had a chance, it was gone with the wind. I couldn't even work on a film set with her as her maid! When she got the offer to do *Queen Bee* I could come with her, work backstage with her, get the smell of theater and acting again. There's no blacklist on Broadway. It was something I wanted to do. It's made me very happy. Now—now this!"

"But there has been trouble, hasn't there? Erratic behavior on her part; missed rehearsals, sometimes drunk, Shields thought, sometimes a brilliant performance, sometimes nothing. I saw a nothing yesterday."

Janet nodded. "It was a big surprise to me, and a puzzle. She'd always been so professional. Mr. Shields assigned Tommy Thompson to try to get her straightened out. He thought it was liquor or drugs. I tried to tell him that I just didn't believe that. Sharon doesn't drink—I mean in the sense of *drinking.* There are drugs all around the film colony and Sharon never expressed anything but contempt for the people who were always working on a high. Finally Tommy got her to go see a doctor friend of his."

"The doctor's name?"

"Paul Wiseman. He has an office over near Radio City. You can find it in the phone book. He seemed like a nice man. I went with Sharon when she went to see him. He thought it was fatigue and stress, and privately he told me he thought it could be acute stage fright."

"A professional like Sharon?"

"Some of the greatest actors have stage fright, from Laurence Olivier on down," Janet said. "Sharon hadn't been onstage for quite a few years. Films are different, you know. If a scene doesn't go well you can take it over and over until it comes out right. An uncertain performance onstage is something you can't take back."

"I think she was on drugs but didn't know it," Quist said.

He told Janet about the Seconal capsules that had been emptied and refilled with something else.

"Oh, my God!" Janet said.

"Where are you living, Janet? Not in the Beaumont to be near her?"

"No. I have a room in a hotel, just a block or so from this theater. Sharon, away from home, is very private about her private life."

"But you had access to her suite at the Beaumont?"

"Access? I'm not sure what you mean."

"You answered her mail, took care of her clothes. Did you have a key to her suite in the Beaumont?"

Janet produced something like a laugh. "Sharon wouldn't give God a key to the place where she lives!"

"Not to a lover? She's supposed to have them by the dozen."

"Not a key to her home base," Janet said. "She always has had to have a place to which she could retreat without fear of any sort of invasion."

"But you don't know for a fact that she didn't change her mind about that rule—just once, perhaps?"

"I don't know it for a fact," Janet said, "but I'd bet my life on it."

"You know she had a gun?"

"Of course. There was no secret about that, even jokes about it. A long time ago she was making a film on location in some small midwestern town. Someone broke into the place where she was staying and tried to rape her. I guess she screamed her head off and got help before it was too late. After that she bought a gun, was licensed to own it, and has had it by her bedside every night of her life since then—when she was alone. She made a point about it, let it be known, made jokes about it. If people knew, it was a way to make her safe."

"So, someone knew she took sleeping pills, that she had

80

a gun, and used both pieces of information to frame her," Quist said. "Can you guess who?"

"I wish to God I could, Mr. Quist. Someone she was involved with sexually? I could give you a list of men in Hollywood, but here in New York . . ." She gave him a helpless shrug. "The list would be so long . . ."

"What about women?" Quist asked. "With her appetite for attractive males and her skill for satisfying it, there must be a lot of girls and women who saw their men charmed away from them. That could add up to an army of haters."

"I suppose," Janet said. She seemed to be thinking of something else.

"There is a woman involved, you know," Quist said. "She phoned the front desk at the Beaumont to tell them she'd heard gunshots."

"Wasn't that the proper thing for someone to do?"

"The guest rooms at the Beaumont are soundproofed. The security people there say this woman who called couldn't have heard shots in another room. If the shots were fired with the door to the hall left open, the maids on duty should have heard the shots. They didn't. It's a strange twist to the whole affair."

"People don't like to get mixed up in things," Janet said. "This woman heard the shots, reported them, but didn't want to be faced by the police and lawyers and God knows who else."

"Maybe," Quist said. He had turned this over and over in his mind. "Maybe she was the killer."

"If she was, why report it? Why not just run?"

"Because she wanted to frame Sharon," Quist said. "After the row in the lobby, the police would be bound to question Sharon when Zuckermann was found shot to death. They'd find the gun that had been used to commit a murder and replaced on Sharon's bedside table. It could be a woman all the way, or a woman acting in cahoots with a man. You answered Sharon's fan mail, you say. Were there ever threatening letters?"

Janet frowned. "There were unfriendly letters," she said. "People who accused her of being an evil woman, religious freaks who threatened her with eternal damnation. There were sex nuts offering to show her what a 'real man' could do for her. But I don't recall any threat of violence."

Quist drew a deep breath. "Well, here we go out into the wild blue yonder."

"If you'd asked me before all this happened whether Sharon could do such a thing, I'd have laughed you out of court, Mr. Quist," Janet said. "But there was the row with Zuckermann; she did take a powerful drug she thought was just a sleeping pill. That could have set her anger to boiling. Not in control of herself she—she could have—"

"But someone had planted the drug in her sleeping capsules," Quist said. "Even if she did the shooting, I think a smart lawyer can get her off—if we can find the person who tampered with her pills. If anyone comes to your mind, Janet, who could have got hold of those pills, please let me know. I'll give you my home phone, my office phone. I could be here at the theater, or at the Beaumont. We've got to find the trail to that person before it gets too cold for us to follow."

When Quist and Janet Lane walked down into the theater proper they saw actors, stage hands, musicians and others connected with the production of *Queen Bee* on stage where Shields and Max Marsden were bringing them up to date on what had happened and what the prospects for the future were. It wasn't, Quist saw, the time to select people at random to talk to who just might come up with some kind of lead. It occurred to him that there might be some current crank mail for Sharon. A psychotic killer might have written some kind of gloating letter to her. The mail, Janet told him, was delivered to Sharon's elegant dressing room, the suite Max Marsden had spent thousands of dollars on to make it satisfactory for a glittering star. Janet led the way down a side aisle, through a stage box, and into the back stage area.

In the dressing room Quist saw stacks of mail on Sharon's dressing table. Janet looked at the letters with a practiced eye.

"A hundred or more," she said. "That's average, normal."

"Take forever to go through them," Quist said. "Can you take a shot at it, Janet? If you need help, I can have someone come over from my office. I've got to go back to the Beaumont to see what's cooking there."

"It could take a couple of hours if I have to read every word," Janet said.

"Every word," Quist said. "I'll get my secretary, Connie Parmalee, over here to help you."

He left her opening the first letter. There was a side door out into the stage door alley and he chose to leave that way. The crowd outside the front of the theater was larger than when he'd arrived. He spoke to the cop who was guarding the mouth of the alley to keep people out, wedged his way through the crowd and headed east toward Broadway and its traffic. People shouted questions at him. What was going on inside? Where was Sharon? Had she really murdered Leon Zuckermann?

He got through the crowd and had gone a few yards toward Broadway when he felt a sharp pain in his head. Something inside his head seemed to explode and he pitched face forward onto the pavement.

Voices shouted. "He's been shot! Someone shot him!"

Quist didn't hear any of them.

2 Out of some dark cave of unconsciousness Quist felt himself swimming to the surface. He was lying down somewhere, and he had a headache to end all headaches. He opened his eyes and found he was in total darkness. He reached up to where his head hurt and his fingers touched some kind of bandage.

"About time you showed some signs of life," a familiar voice said.

Quist opened his mouth to speak and didn't recognize the sound of his own voice. "Mark?"

Lieutenant Kreevich's voice was unmistakable. "In the flesh," it said, accompanied by a little chuckle.

"Where are we?"

"At St. Clare's Hospital," the detective said. "How do you feel?"

"Awful," Quist said. "Why the hell don't they turn on some lights? How did I get here?"

"Ambulance. You remember what happened?"

Quist tried to penetrate the fog. He had come out of the stage door at the Tempest Theater, walked out the alley, headed east toward Broadway through a crowd of people— and there it ended.

"Someone shot you," Kreevich said.

"Will you, for Christ's sake, turn on a light!" Quist said.

Kreevich's voice had a harsh quality to it. "It's two o'clock in the afternoon, Julian. The sunlight is streaming through the windows of this room."

Quist raised his hands and discovered that there was no bandage over his eyes. "Oh, my God!" he said.

"Take it easy, chum," Kreevich said. His strong hand closed over Quist's wrist. "I want the doctor to tell you how it is, but I'll try—in a completely unprofessional way."

"I can't see, Mark!"

"The bullet was fired from behind you," Kreevich said. "You could call it a miracle. It plowed a little furrow from the back of your head right along one side of it to your forehead. It didn't penetrate more than a fraction of an inch, or you'd be knocking on the Pearly Gates."

"*I can't see*, Mark!"

"They know," Kreevich said. "Preliminary X-rays don't show any serious damage. They hope it's just a temporary paralysis of your eye functions."

"They *hope?*" Quist's voice was unsteady.

"When you're in a little better shape, they'll do a more extensive examination. If you'll stay quiet for a few minutes, I'll try to find the doctor for you."

"Oh, my God!" Quist said.

"Lydia's just outside. She'd like to see you. Your friend Dan Garvey is with her."

Dan Garvey was one of Quist's partners in Julian Quist Associates.

"They—they know?" Quist asked.

"Yes. We've all been told to be optimistic, Julian. They just want you to know they're here, standing by."

"How—why are you here, Mark?"

"It was an attempted homicide, chum. It may be connected with a murder I'm investigating. And, just in passing, you're a friend I care about."

"Have they got the person who shot me?" Quist asked.

85

"No. The cop in charge wants to talk to you about it. So do I, when you feel up to it. Let me get the doctor, first, to tell you exactly what your story is. Lydia and Dan are awfully anxious to see you."

Quist felt the muscles of his jaw tighten. "Am I—am I tough to look at?"

Again there was the sound of a chuckle in Kreevich's voice. "They've shaved one side of your head," he said. "Shave the other side and you could act as a stand-in for Telly Savalas."

"God knows I don't want to be alone," Quist said. "Not while I can't see."

"Could be a temporary blessing," Kreevich said, his voice cold. "It's an ugly world."

Panic was not an emotion Quist had ever felt before. He had never before doubted his own competence to deal with a crisis. He heard a door open and close. Was that Kreevich going—or someone coming? His fingernails dug into the palms of his hands. Would he be able to endure this? Would he be able to face helplessness?

The door across the room opened again. He lifted up on an elbow and stared at—darkness!

"Julian?"

He thought he might burst into tears. "Oh, God, it's you, luv!"

And then Lydia was beside him, her cheek pressed against his, whispering words that he couldn't really hear. He put an arm around her shoulders. He could imagine how she looked, her eyes probably red from weeping.

"You smell so damn good," he said.

"You idiot!"

"I'd better keep my distance," Dan Garvey's voice said. Garvey, a former professional football star, was Quist's partner and closest friend. Quist could visualize him, dark, intense, with a brilliant white smile. "Dan's threatening smile," Quist called it. When that smile was aimed at you, look out!

"Everyone has a thousand questions to ask you," Garvey said.

"And I don't have any answers," Quist said. "I didn't see anyone, didn't hear anything. Just suddenly something exploded inside my head—and that was that."

"No one shouted at you, warned you?"

"Everyone was shouting questions at me. I'd just come out of the theater," Quist said. "I didn't pay any attention. I was just walking away and—boom!"

The door opened at the far end of the room. Quist moved, but Lydia held him close. "It's Dr. Jorgensen," she whispered to him.

Was this the way it was going to be forever, Lydia seeing for him, caring for him like a useless child?

"I'm Carl Jorgensen, Mr. Quist," a pleasant, baritone voice said. "I'm delighted to see you showing signs of life."

Lydia tried to move away from him but Quist held her close. "You've met Miss Morton and Mr. Garvey, Doctor?"

"Yes. We've met and talked," the doctor said.

"So talk to me," Quist said. He could imagine a black-robed judge about to say, "I sentence you to . . ."

"It's like the old joke," Dr. Jorgensen said. "I have good news for you and bad news for you. The good news is that you had a miraculous escape. The shot was obviously fired from directly behind you, and the bullet just scraped the side of your head. If it had been fired at an angle it would have probably penetrated and that would have spelled finish. The bullet, as it scraped the side of your head, could have fragmented and left pieces imbedded in your skull. X-rays show that it didn't. You couldn't have been luckier."

"I can't see, Doctor."

"I know. That's the bad news."

A middle-aged man, Quist thought from the sound of his

87

voice. A lot of vitality that somehow inspired confidence. Quist felt a faint chill run over him. Was he going to have to make judgments about people from the sound of them instead of from seeing them, watching them?

"But I think not too bad," Dr. Jorgensen said. "When you can see again, I'll draw you a diagram. Simply, the bullet grazed your skull very close to the nerve centers that control your sight. Those nerves are paralyzed—temporarily, I think."

"How temporarily?" Quist asked.

Quist could visualize the doctor's shrug. "A day, a week, a month. We should be able to tell more accurately after we can make a few more tests."

"Meanwhile?"

"Meanwhile there's nothing else the matter with you," the doctor said. "We'll take the stitches out of your wound in a few days. You can go home tomorrow."

"And wait," Quist said.

"Mr. Quist, you could turn over in bed ten minutes from now and see."

"Or ten weeks from now?"

"Maybe."

"Or never?"

"I think not 'never,'" the doctor said, "unless we discover damage we haven't found so far."

"Isn't that marvelous, darling?" Lydia whispered.

"And meanwhile I'll find the sonofabitch who did this to you, Julian," Dan Garvey said. Quist guessed the threatening smile was there.

Later Quist was to realize that Kreevich was acting as a friend, not a policeman. The detective had come back into the room while the doctor was still there.

"Is there any reason why we shouldn't talk to him about serious business, Doctor?" Kreevich asked.

Serious business! Didn't the damn fool know that he couldn't see?

"No reason I can think of," Dr. Jorgensen said. "Might help take his mind off his troubles."

"Sorry, Julian," Kreevich said. "I've got Sergeant Hanson with me. He's in charge of what happened to you."

"What happened to me is that I'm blind!" Quist said. He sounded to himself like a querulous old woman.

"The doctor assures us it's only temporary," Sergeant Hanson's unfamiliar voice said. "Sorry to bother you now, but you know how it is—while the iron's hot."

Lydia's cool hand touched Quist's cheek. "You don't mind if Dan and I stay, do you, Mark? Then Julian won't have to tell it to us all over again."

"I wish to God I had something to tell," Quist said. "I was walking away from the theater and some kook shot me!"

"Stay, of course," Kreevich said. "Your ball game, Sergeant."

"We have a couple of hundred witnesses, none of whom saw anything," Sergeant Hanson said. "Some of them say they saw you come out of the stage door alley, asked you some questions. When you didn't answer, walked away, they turned back toward the theater where their interest was centered. Three or four of them say they heard the shot, but they were looking the other way. Someone on the fringe of the crowd saw you fall, saw the blood on your head, and then they all crowded around you. The person who shot you may have slipped away, or may have stayed right there."

"I had my back to whoever fired the shot," Quist said. "I didn't see anything!" I may never see anything again, he thought. He tried to imagine what Hanson looked like. Gravelly voice, probably a big man, overweight, just another thickheaded cop.

"The lieutenant tells me you are working on a theory that

89

differs from his about the Zuckermann murder," Hanson said.

"I hope he told you that Sharon Ladd didn't shoot me," Quist said. "You still have her under arrest, don't you, Mark?"

"She didn't shoot you," Kreevich said, quietly. "She's still in the hospital facilities at the Beaumont."

"You went to the theater to talk to people there," Hanson said. "How many people know what you were thinking?"

Quist tried to get his mind back to that visit. "I talked to Max Marsden, my friend, the producer. I talked to Larry Shields, the director. I talked to Janet Lane, Sharon's secretary, dresser, friend."

"That's all?" Hanson asked.

"That's all. I left Janet Lane going through Sharon's mail. I hoped there might be some kind of crank letter there."

"It doesn't much matter that you only talked to those three people, does it?" Kreevich asked, in a cold, impersonal voice. "When you left the theater Marsden and Shields had the whole company onstage—actors, musicians, stagehands, box-office people, even the kid who goes for coffee—telling them you had evidence that Sharon was innocent and that she might be able to come back to work. So everyone connected with the *Queen Bee* operation knew what you were up to."

"I suppose," Quist said.

"You wouldn't make a very good cop, Julian, letting every possible suspect know what you were aiming at," Kreevich said.

"Most of the crowd outside the theater evaporated when the ambulance had taken you away, Mr. Quist, and the police arrived," Hanson said. "People don't like to get involved in violence. But Max Marsden told us why you were there, which got us to Lieutenant Kreevich. We searched the people on the outside who hung around, and we searched everyone in the theater, and the theater itself. No gun. That's not a hundred percent accurate. There was a gun in the box office, always kept there. It hadn't been fired recently or cleaned recently. Probably not the right caliber, although we haven't found the bullet that was fired at you."

"Down a drain or through an open office window," Kreevich said.

"That's where the gun probably is," Hanson said. "Down a street drain into a sewer and long gone."

"How could a man shoot off a gun in a crowd of people and nobody see it?" Dan Garvey's voice asked.

"People making noise," Hanson said. "People shouting questions at Quist, a man who'd just come out of the theater; normal street traffic, cabs and trucks blowing their horns to get people back onto the sidewalk where they'd spilled out into the street. In that kind of confusion a gunshot doesn't sound like an explosion, you know. At the most a car backfire; a handgun wouldn't make that much noise. It's not surprising nobody identified the sound when it was made. Quist falling down, the blood, that they saw."

"But people were yelling Julian had been shot," Garvey persisted.

"The world we live in," Hanson said. "What else brings a man down with blood streaming out of the side of his head?"

"It could have been someone who followed Julian out of the theater, or someone who was waiting for him in the crowd outside," Garvey said.

"Needle-in-a-haystack department," Kreevich said. "Someone just walked away with the gun in his pocket before the cops arrived. Just some crazy who took a shot at a likely target."

"You're saying you don't think there's any connection between this and the Zuckermann business?" Garvey asked. He sounded angry.

"I'm saying that," Kreevich said.

91

"Oh, my God, Mark," Garvey said.

"I'm saying that's what I'm saying," Kreevich said. "I'm not saying that's what I'm thinking."

Quist turned his head toward the sound of Kreevich's voice. If he could only *see* his friend, he might understand better what this kind of double-talk meant.

"What are you thinking, Mark?" he asked.

"As I told you a little while back, I'm thinking there *may* be a connection between what happened to you and the murder of Leon Zuckermann. But it's got to prove out, Julian."

"But Sharon Ladd is off the hook?" Quist asked.

"There are hooks and hooks," Kreevich's flat, cold voice said. This wasn't Kreevich the friend, Quist thought. This was Kreevich the cop. He didn't have to see what he guessed was a rock-hard face, the mouth a thin, tight slit.

"Hooks and hooks—meaning what?" Quist asked.

"I tend to believe that you were right about what happened, Julian," the detective said. "A frame-up. Someone tampered with Sharon's sleeping pills. She took a powerful drug she didn't know she was taking and passed out. Someone had a way to get into her suite at the Beaumont, knew that gun would be on her bedside table, took it, went down to the twelfth floor and shot Zuckermann, went back to the thirtieth floor and replaced the gun on Sharon's bedside table."

"And then called the desk to say there'd been a shooting on the twelfth floor," Quist said. "A woman."

"Could be," Kreevich said. "Could be the woman was working with the killer. When he'd finished his job and framed Sharon, he let his woman accomplice know. She phoned the hotel, from God knows where."

"So if you buy all that, Sharon Ladd's free and clear."

"I said it could be that way," Kreevich said. "But if it is, she's still not off the hook."

"Legal mumbo-jumbo," Garvey said.

"No," Kreevich said brusquely.

"But surely you can set her free," Quist said.

"What do you think the killer was after?" Kreevich asked. "Do you think Zuckermann was his primary target, or do you think Sharon is? They'd been working on Sharon for some three weeks, drugging her, getting her to screw up rehearsals. I keep saying 'they' because I can't shake the notion that it's not just one person. They are out to destroy Sharon. Then Zuckermann shows up. Did he come to the Beaumont, where Sharon was living, by design or by accident? In any case, he came there, ran into Sharon in the lobby, and an angry scene followed. These people, 'they,' knew so much intimate detail about Sharon—her use of sleeping pills, the gun. They saw a way to get her, but good. They gave her time to take her pills, pass out, and then they went to work. That has to be proved, but let's say it's so."

"If it's so, she's in the clear," Garvey said.

"And their target once more," Kreevich said. "As long as they think I'm about to waltz her down the aisle to the grand jury they'll let her alone, let me do their dirty work for them. Let them know that I no longer suspect her, don't plan to bring charges against her, and they'll find some new way to attack her, destroy her. Like I said, off one hook and onto another. So, what I say publicly may not be what I think privately. It's a way to keep Sharon Ladd safe—or at least safer—until we can reach out and grab the real killer."

"Meanwhile they can concentrate on Julian," Garvey said. "They may not miss the next time."

"Julian is hurt, blinded," Kreevich said, in that same cold voice. "He'll stop playing cops and robbers. He's no longer a danger to them."

"You're a pretty cold-blooded jerk, Mark," Garvey said.

"Oh, come off it, Dan!" Kreevich said. "I'm telling you what I'm saying to the press, not what I'm thinking or feeling. Sharon Ladd, I'll tell them, is still the number one suspect in the Zuckermann murder. As long as they believe that, they'll let me kill her for them. As long as they think Julian is incapacitated and concerned only with himself, they'll let him alone."

"God knows there's no way I can be of any use," Quist said.

Kreevich's voice had a whiplash sting to it. "I never thought of you as a quitter, Julian."

"Mark!" It was a protest from Lydia.

"People are going to feel sorry for you, chum," Kreevich said, ignoring Lydia. "Half the world knows what you were up to. They'll want to come to you with gossip, with any kind of guesses they care to make, with what they know about Sharon, about Zuckermann, about anyone else in the past or present. Information can come your way that no aggressive police investigation will ever uncover. You can play a big hand in this game, Julian, unless you choose to feel sorry for yourself and give up."

There was a kind of shocked silence in the room. Quist felt Lydia's hand tighten in his. "Thanks, Mark," he said.

"For what?" Kreevich asked.

"For pointing out to me where I was heading," Quist said.

3 The press, the radio, and
television had a mass of contradictory statements by the
end of the day. Sharon Ladd and Leon Zuckermann had
been feeding the world stories about themselves for some
years. Their marriage, their divorce, the property suits
filed by Zuckermann against the lady, had provided a field
day for gossip columnists and movie historians for the last
six or seven years. The bloody climax in the Beaumont
Hotel brought the past charging back into the present. The
shooting-down of Julian Quist outside the Tempest Theater
added spice to an already sensational event.

Julian Quist was not as famous a figure in the public eye
as Sharon Ladd and Leon Zuckermann, but the ladies and
gentlemen of the media knew him equally well as a topflight public relations expert, constantly in touch with them
about people and business ventures he'd been engaged to
promote. There was no way in the world to keep what he'd
been up to at the Tempest from reaching the reporters.
Dozens of people involved with the *Queen Bee* production
were eager to talk about what they'd been told by Max
Marsden and Larry Shields. The news in this was that
Quist, a highly respected and responsible man, was working on a totally different answer to the Zuckermann murder
from the one offered by the New York police and the District Attorney's office. Quist had been shot, it was assumed,

to prevent him from pursuing his theory, which tended to make it seem more believable. Reporters who had been prepared to hang Sharon Ladd before she was ever brought to trial, suddenly had doubts and found themselves looking in other directions for answers. Quist, in the hospital, was suddenly the center of attention. Reporters wanted to talk to him, hoping for some lead from him to a different answer to a murder. What they didn't know, crowding in and around the hospital, waiting for the doctors to give them permission to talk with Quist, was that he was no longer there. Kreevich, talking one way and thinking another, had decided there was no way to keep this mass intrusion away from his friend. Dr. Jorgensen had agreed that there was no physical reason why he couldn't be moved. He, the doctor, would visit Quist at home, and it would be a day or two before major tests would have to be made at the hospital.

So it was that Quist was spirited away in an unmarked police car and taken home to his apartment on Beekman Place, with Lydia and Dan Garvey to care for him. Attendants in the building were enlisted in the cause and a plainclothes police officer was placed on duty to guard against anyone who might try too persistently to get to Lydia for any information she might have.

Somehow, just being at home helped to quell the deepseated panic that had been eating at Quist. The chair he sat in was familiar. The voices around him were familiar. The coffee Lydia made him, laced with brandy, warmed and cheered him. Eventually Lydia was sitting beside him, her hand in his, and he felt almost safe.

Except that he couldn't see her, couldn't see the lights of the city that blinked outside the windows. He couldn't *see!*

The other thing that wouldn't give Quist any kind of peace was the telephone. It rang and rang. Reporters who hoped someone connected with Quist would be there to answer questions wouldn't let up. Friends, concerned for Quist, kept calling to ask how he was. Garvey handled the calls, brisk and unfriendly to reporters. Quist was still at the hospital! No, he couldn't have visitors. Garvey didn't know how soon he would be able to talk. He had been blinded by the gunshot wound and there was no way to guess when the doctors would let him be interviewed. Friends were handled a little more gently. Quist was still at the hospital, temporarily blinded but otherwise not seriously hurt. As soon as there was some positive report from the doctors, Garvey would pass it along.

"One thing that should make you feel good," Garvey said, after one of those calls, "you've got more friends than most people."

And the phone rang again.

The voice was unfamiliar to Garvey. "This is Charles Tyler, Bud Tyler, calling," the voice said.

"Tyler?"

Quist sat up straight when he heard the name mentioned. He made a gesture with his hand to suggest that Garvey keep talking.

"I'm Dan Garvey, Julian's partner," Garvey said.

"I am Sharon Ladd's last husband," Tyler said. "Quist came to see me yesterday. I think I may have something that will be useful to him."

"You know what happened to him?" Garvey asked.

"I have a round-the-clock radio," Tyler said.

"Well, he's in the hospital," Garvey said, "not able to have visitors or talk to anyone."

"Look, Mr. Garvey, about a year ago I spent two months at St. Clare's. While I was there I made friends with a nurse. She tells me Quist isn't there any longer. I assume that he's at his home there with you."

"Damn!" Garvey said.

"She tells me that he's been temporarily blinded by the

shot that was fired at him. I take it he couldn't come to see me?"

"No way," Garvey said.

"Ask him if I could come to see him. It might help if I could give him a clue as to who tried to get him."

"Hold the fort," Garvey said. He covered the mouthpiece of the phone with his hand and conveyed the gist of the conversation to Quist.

"He can't get here," Quist said. "He's anchored to a wheelchair."

"Tell him I can get there," Tyler said on the phone. "I have a friend who carts me around town in his car. And tell Quist he can rest easy. I won't tell anyone I've found him."

"Your friend?"

"You can count on him to keep his mouth shut."

Once more Garvey told Quist what was being said.

"Tell him to come," Quist said. "Tell him I'm sorry I can't make it easier for him."

"What can he know?" Garvey asked when he'd told Tyler to come and put down the phone.

"He's made a life study of Sharon Ladd," Quist said.

"You get to know people well, either personally or through a history passed on to you by friends you trust, and then something happens and you just know it couldn't have happened that way," Bud Tyler said.

He had arrived at Beekman Place in a car with a special door that accommodated his wheelchair. The building attendants had been alerted by Garvey, and the plainclothes cop on duty. The young man who helped Tyler out of his car and escorted him into the building lobby had taken off, leaving Tyler on his own. He was, to the complete surprise of the cop and the doorman, wearing a black silk mask over what they couldn't know was a revoltingly scarred face. He

98

handled his wheelchair with almost-magical skills, across the lobby, into the elevator and up to Quist's floor where Garvey, alerted from the lobby, was waiting for him.

"The mask may be a little flamboyant, but I wouldn't want you and Quist's lady distracted by staring at what's behind it. I'm not pretty, Mr. Garvey."

"Come in," Garvey said.

Tyler wheeled himself into the living room. Quist was sitting in an armchair, a pair of heavy black-lensed glasses covering his eyes.

"Bud?" Quist asked.

"Hell, Julian," Tyler said. "I'm wearing a mask over my face. I didn't want your friends gagging while they looked at me."

"We're both in hiding," Quist said.

"I was shocked to hear what had happened to you," Tyler said. He was looking at the beautiful woman standing by Quist's chair. "You must be Miss Morton."

"I'm sorry," Quist said. "I guess you forget your manners when you're not all in one piece."

"Yes, I'm Lydia Morton," Lydia said. "Could I get a drink, some coffee, Mr. Tyler?"

"After we've talked I'd enjoy something," Tyler said. He made his little speech about getting to know people so well that you know things couldn't have happened the way they're described.

"You're talking about Sharon?" Quist asked.

"I agreed with you yesterday, Julian. No way in the world she would have knowingly murdered Zuckermann."

"What do you mean 'knowingly'?" Garvey said.

"Drugs that blacked her out," Tyler said. He moved his chair a little closer to Quist. "I didn't come here just to exchange theories with you, Julian." The black mask turned so that it was clear he meant to include them all. "You all have to understand something. I love Sharon, I won her, I lost her, and I still love her. I have watched over her for the last two years, ready to do anything at all that would be any use to her. She has a problem that, sooner or later, was bound to bring her world clattering down around her. I wanted to be able to help pick up the pieces when that time came. That's why I'm here."

"She didn't desert you when you had trouble," Quist said.

"I know," Tyler said, "but I owe her a great deal more than that. For about six months she gave me a happiness I'd never had before and will never have again." His voice was unsteady for a moment. Then he seemed to straighten up in his wheelchair. "So, facts," he said. "I've spent the last hours on the phone to the West Coast. I have friends out there, and so does Sharon. Maybe I should begin by telling you that Leon Zuckermann has been a part of my life ever since Sharon and I first got together. The man was a monster."

"But a genius at film making," Quist said.

"Yes, you've got to give him that," Tyler said. "But as a human being, his only genius was for cruelty, a capacity for degrading decent people, and an almost savage hunger for revenge against anyone who crossed him or made him look anything less than godlike. He never forgave or forgot anyone who did anything to damage his ego."

"Janet Lane told me a little something about that," Quist said. "A Hollywood blacklist . . ."

"Poor Janet," Tyler said. "She gave in to him, foolishly, in the beginning and then—then she said 'no.' But that isn't why he's hated and hounded her all this time. He might have forgotten her, not thought it was worth the trouble to keep on standing in her way, but Sharon befriended her. In the end he knew that the game Sharon played with him was meant to punish him for what he'd done to Janet. Sharon destroyed his ego, and he hated her and anyone connected with her with a passion. I don't think he has spent a waking moment since Sharon walked out on him, laughing at him, on the day of their wedding, without scheming for some way to inflict an intolerable punishment on her."

"But he's the one who's dead!" Garvey said.

"He was able to blacklist Janet Lane," Quist said. "Why didn't he wreck Sharon's career?"

"She was too big a star," Tyler said. "She could make too much money for too many other big shots in Hollywood. He had to get at her some other way."

"So he arranged to get himself killed in order to get even with her?" Garvey said. His laugh was impatient. Quist guessed the threatening smile was there. "Some revenge!"

"Let Bud tell it, Dan," Quist said. He could guess how Dan and Lydia looked, but even if he were not blind the black silk mask would have hidden Tyler's emotions from him.

"It goes back to the death of Billy Lockman, Sharon's third husband, the one before Zuckermann," Tyler said.

"Some kind of barroom brawl," Quist said.

"A Texas he-man," Tyler said. Quist heard a note of contempt in the voice. "So rich it came out of his ears; blond, handsome, noisy—and like most of us who have been hooked by Sharon, in love with her forever." It was there again, the slight unsteadiness of voice.

"I never met Billy," Tyler went on, "but I heard about him from Sharon and from dozens of others after he was gunned down."

"They never arrested the man who killed him, did they?" Quist asked.

"But that's where the story begins," Tyler said. He drew a deep breath, and Lydia and Garvey, who could see him, saw his hands tighten on the arms of his wheelchair. "Billy was living on his ranch in Texas. I think they call it a 'spread' down there. He and Sharon had been married for about a year, which is par for the course. She was away somewhere, making a picture. Word came from everywhere that she was marrying Zuckermann. Billy went off like a rocket. He and Sharon weren't divorced! There was no way she could marry someone else—no way Billy was going to let it happen.

"What Billy didn't know was that she'd gotten a quickie in Reno or someplace. Maybe Mexico. Billy charged up from Texas to Hollywood to rescue his woman from the dragon!" Tyler's chuckle was wry. "He found the Zuckermann establishment in some disarray. The bride had walked out on the groom, without even taking off a stocking for his benefit. Billy laughed himself sick when he heard. He was given the heave-ho by Zuckermann's people and an attack dog was turned loose on him. Back in Texas, Billy spread the word like a forest fire. Zuckermann had been given the business by Sharon to get even for what he'd done to her friend, Janet Lane. It was a nightly joke in the bars. Sharon hadn't even let Zuckermann touch her hand, and she'd taken him for a fortune in film contracts he'd have to honor, like it or not. Zuckermann was a laughing-stock in Texas."

"But Billy had still lost his woman," Garvey said.

"But not to a greasy monster like Zuckermann," Tyler said. "Then one night a stranger appeared in one of the bars Billy was haunting since his troubles began. He laughed at Billy, indulged in a lot of insulting remarks about Sharon, until Billy blew his stack. There were suddenly guns, and Billy got it—right between the eyes. In the excitement, the stranger managed to get away. He was never caught, never identified."

"So—another Texas soap opera," Garvey said.

"We tried," Tyler said.

"We?" Quist asked.

"Sharon and I," Tyler said. "You see, Sharon thought,

102

and she convinced me, that Zuckermann was behind what happened to Billy."

"Zuckermann!"

"Never forgives, never forgets," Tyler said. "Billy had spread the word all over Texas—all over Hollywood—that there had been no wedding night. That Zuckermann had been played for a sucker by Sharon. Sharon believed from the very first that Zuckermann had hired a hit man to go down to Texas and polish Billy off."

"Oh, wow!" Garvey said.

"The story I heard from Janet Lane was that Billy drew first on the man who killed him," Quist said.

"It may be so," Tyler said. "Billy drew a gun to threaten the man who was tormenting him. The man was waiting for just that. While Billy was shouting at him and waving his gun the man shot him, from where he was sitting—or standing. Probably through his coat pocket. He never showed a gun. In a matter of seconds, while the place was in an uproar, the man was gone."

"No one could describe him?" Quist asked.

"Oh, there were descriptions," Tyler said. "The police circulated an artist's drawing, made from those descriptions, all over the country. Tall, dark man with a reddish beard. Nothing ever came of it. Whoever he was, he got away with it scot-free."

"Where does that get us?" Quist asked.

"A possible picture of Zuckermann and how he could function," Tyler said.

"But not proved," Quist said.

"Sharon and I had met, had loved, and were married," Tyler said. A hard, cold quality had crept into his voice. "I should have been warned, I suppose. There had been three real husbands before me—and Zuckermann, legally but not ever really a husband. Sharon never promised me anything she couldn't give. She warned me that when she

103

was away from me—and our careers would separate us from time to time—she wouldn't be able to resist what came her way in terms of sexual excitement. I didn't believe it. What we had was too perfect, I thought. Temptation would come and she would find it easy to resist, I thought. But it happened. She was honest about it. She told me—some character in London where she was making a film. Some British lord, an officer and a gentleman for God's sake!" Quist could hear the pain in Tyler's voice. "I tried to forgive her. I—I tried to tell myself that when we were apart it was something I'd have to face. It was tough, but I thought I could survive it. I was committed to drive in a stock car classic in Carolina. She was working in Hollywood in a film studio there. I got down to Carolina and after a couple of days of pre-race preparations I got an unsigned telegram from Hollywood. It informed me that Sharon was in the hay with a film star. I called her on the phone. She admitted it, but swore on everything she held dear that it was over. She suggested to me that the telegram meant that Zuckermann was at work again."

"You believed her?" Quist asked.

"Yes, I believed that she had ended the affair. The Zuckermann thing seemed far-fetched to me, though it wouldn't have been unlike him. Then came the day of the race and I smashed up. You've seen what I look like, Quist. You know that I can't move out of this damned chair. That was the end. I knew. Sharon could never spend the rest of her life with a crippled gargoyle. I couldn't ask it of her."

"And she didn't offer?"

"Oh, she offered, but I wouldn't hear of it. I knew she couldn't make it work, even if she wanted to. I couldn't live with a wife who'd be making love with every attractive man who came her way. I used the telegram as a grounds for divorce."

"Cut off your own nose to spite your face," Garvey said.

"What face? You want to look, Mr. Garvey?"

"What has this got to do with Zuckermann?" Quist interrupted quickly.

"My crew in the race track in Carolina, my mechanics, went over the wreckage of my car," Tyler said. "The steering mechanism—someone had sawed through one of the cables. It was a clean cut, no chance of a wear-out. It had given way on the first sharp turn at high speed. It wasn't an accident. Well, while I was in the hospital I got a note, unsigned, from Hollywood. 'This is what you get for messing around with a lady who never belonged to you.' Do you wonder that I started to think about Zuckermann?"

"You'd never harmed him," Garvey said.

"But Sharon had cared for me! It was meant to hurt her, and to hell with me," Tyler said. His voice lowered. "I hired private detectives, told them my suspicion, but they never came up with anything. Whoever sawed through the cable on my car disappeared just as completely as the man with the red beard had in Texas. This time we had no description, no nothing. The only thing we ever got was that the night of the day I cracked up Zuckermann gave a big champagne party at Romanoff's in Hollywood. It was, he told his friends, 'to celebrate a success.' He'd just finished a big film, and that was what people thought it was about. I never believed it. He was celebrating my being smashed to pieces on a Carolina race track."

"Is it possible, Tyler," Garvey asked in a flat voice, "that you're living in a fantasy world?"

"You didn't know Zuckermann," Tyler said. "I told you I'd spent most of the last twenty-four hours on the phone to people in Hollywood. You care to hear what I came up with?"

"Please," Quist said.

"Sharon's been in rehearsal for about three weeks," Tyler said. "The gossip columnists have let her alone during that time, but not Zuckermann. He's been telling people all over Hollywood that things were going badly for Sharon, that she was about to have one of the biggest flops in history. He seemed to have a detailed account of what was going on. He spread the news that she couldn't remember lines, was drinking, taking drugs, messing around with new lovers. From what I gathered it was as though he was there, watching."

"Someone reporting to him?"

"That's what I think," Tyler said. "A couple of days ago, he gave another of his parties. He told everyone there that he was coming to New York to see the first preview performance at the Tempest, scheduled for day after tomorrow. It was going to give him the utmost pleasure to see Sharon cut down to size. And so he came, having reserved a room at the Beaumont so he could watch every move she made. By a coincidence they ran into each other in the lobby just as he was checking in. He told her why he was there and she slugged him with her handbag."

"And a few hours later he was shot with her gun," Garvey said. Quist guessed again at the threatening smile. "Are you suggesting he planned to have her shoot him as a way to deliver a final punishment for what she did to him?"

"If it amuses you to make jokes, I don't suppose I can stop you," Tyler said.

"What do you really think, Bud?" Quist asked.

"Someone doctored Sharon's Seconal capsules," Tyler said. "Not Zuckermann, he was in Hollywood. But someone working for him? Someone working for him may have killed Billy Lockman. Someone working for him may have sawed through the steering cable on my racing car. Is it hard to imagine that someone working for him drugged Sharon?"

"And that someone working for him took a shot at Julian?" Garvey asked, angry impatience still there in his voice. "Zuckermann was dead when that shot was fired. Someone working for Zuckermann took Sharon's gun and

106

shot his boss with it? You've got a hell of a lot of untangling to do, Tyler."

"I don't think that's too hard," Tyler said.

"Only if you've decided that Sharon, under the influence of drugs, killed Zuckermann," Quist said. He wished to God he could see Tyler's reaction to that.

"I've thought about it and thought about it," Tyler said. "It could be that way, you know? Zuckermann and his man here couldn't have foreseen the row in the lobby; couldn't have foreseen what a drugged Sharon's reaction would be after that row. But certainly, Julian, if that's how it was, a good lawyer can get her off. She wasn't responsible for what she did. Zuckermann set up his own disaster."

"So from a slab in the morgue Zuckermann ordered his man to polish off Julian?" Garvey asked, still angry.

"More jokes," Tyler said. He was beginning to react with an anger of his own. "Zuckermann's man is on his own now. If we can nail him for doctoring Sharon's sleeping pills, the police and the District Attorney would have a case against him—possibly even a murder charge. As of this morning Julian seemed to be the only person sniffing around at the truth. Zuckermann's man, protecting himself now, tried to silence him."

"And missed by a fraction of an inch," Garvey said.

"And that's not a joke," Tyler said. "From what I heard from my contacts in Hollywood, I have the impression that Zuckermann had an hour-by-hour, day-by-day report on how Sharon was doing—how his scheme was working. That suggests to me someone in the *Queen Bee* company was watching every step of the way and reporting back to Zuckermann."

"Now gone with the wind," Quist said, "like the man with the red beard in Texas, the man with the metal saw in Carolina."

"Maybe not," Tyler said. "To disappear now would be to

107

point a finger at himself. He's been working there for almost three weeks now, an actor, a musician, a technician. Someone in on all the rehearsals reporting on how Sharon was fouling things up. Take off now and the hounds would be after him."

"So he just sits there, waiting for Max Marsden to close the show, when they can all disband and disappear without arousing any suspicion," Garvey said.

"That's the way it seems to me," Tyler said.

It was, Quist thought, like hearing the sound track of a film without being able to see the pictures. If he could have seen Tyler while he was talking it could have added so much—the movements in the wheelchair, the nervous use of hands, the tensing and relaxing of muscles. He had never realized before how much the visual clues went toward authenticating the spoken words.

One thing about Tyler's visit. It had helped him, for a while, to overcome the terrible panic that had been with him ever since he'd regained consciousness in the hospital. Lydia had made drinks and all of them sat, Quist in darkness, discussing what their next move should be.

"We must lay this out for Mark Kreevich," Quist said. "He has police contacts everywhere. Take any one of these things—the murder of Billy Lockman, the sabotaging of your car in Carolina, Bud, the murder of Zuckermann and the attack on me—and it would be hard to make any one of them stick. But put them all together and you just can't ignore the connections."

"All out of the same twisted mind," Lydia said, speaking almost at the same time. She was sitting next to Quist, her hand resting on his. She knew instinctively how important that contact was to him. This meeting should end. He should be resting.

"So, we buy it," Garvey said. "That means the answer is somewhere at the Tempest Theater. Do we leave it to the cops, or do we go after it ourselves?"

"If Julian goes after it, he may be a target again," Lydia said. Her hand tightened on Quist's.

"Do you imagine, luv, that anything could be more gratifying than to have a part in catching him?" Quist asked. "I think one of you will have to take me to the theater in the morning. Janet Lane, Thompson, the stage manager who was helpful to Sharon—one of them may know of someone in the company who had a contact with Zuckermann at some other time."

"Could help you, or warn a killer that he can't afford to allow you another hour of time," Garvey said. "Leave it to me and Tyler, Julian. At least we can—can see what's coming!"

"It may be good enough to guess what's coming," Quist said, his voice cold. "Try to reach Kreevich on the phone, Lydia. Before I call it a day I'd like his permission to talk to Sharon."

"Julian! You can't go over to the Beaumont!"

"Why not? I have the two best guide dogs in captivity, don't I?"

"Wait till tomorrow!"

"Tomorrow it's the Tempest Theater—and a killer," Quist said. "Call Mark, please, Lydia."

Kreevich took some persuading. His concern was for Quist, not only that he wasn't up to traveling around so soon, but that appearing at the Beaumont would reveal the deception about his still being at the hospital. Lydia explained to him about Bud Tyler's visit and that there might be new evidence which could help support Sharon.

"As for his being up to it," Lydia told the lieutenant, "I

felt as you do when he first suggested it. I think, though, that being involved may help him to keep his mind off what must be driving him up the wall."

"He's still not seeing anything?"

"Nothing."

Kreevich made his decision. "I'll send a police car for you," he said. "We'll drive him into the basement garage at the hotel and take him up to the hotel hospital on the service elevator. Not much chance that he'll be seen or recognized that way."

It was a little after nine o'clock in the evening when Quist, Lydia, and Dan Garvey were escorted into the hospital unit at the hotel by a plainclothes cop. Quist, holding tightly to Garvey's arm, heard the little cry of shocked surprise that came from Sharon.

"Oh, Julian! I heard on the radio. Oh, my God, what a thing to happen to you."

He could imagine her, staring wide-eyed at him, his eyes hidden behind the black glasses, the shaved area and the strip of adhesive tape on the side of his head.

"They tell me it's temporary," he said. "I had to talk to you, Sharon."

Someone placed a chair for him. He realized that she wasn't in bed any longer. She was suddenly kneeling beside the chair, taking his hand in hers.

"Bad luck for you when you got involved with me," she said. "I'm always bad luck to people who try to do anything for me."

"Nonsense," he said. "I'm here because Bud Tyler came to me with a long, involved story. I hope you can help us make some sense out of it. Bud, by the way, wants to help in any way he can."

"Poor Bud! If he'd never met me—"

"Just listen to what he had to tell me."

He outlined for her the Zuckermann saga as Tyler had presented it, the suspicion that Zuckermann had been responsible for the murder of Billy Lockman, for the sabotaging of Bud's race car, and probably the substitution of a potent drug for her sleeping pills.

"Revenge that finally backfired on him," Quist said.

"Bud thinks I killed Leon while I was drugged?" Sharon asked. Some of the vitality had gone out of her voice.

"It's possible," Quist said. "But if we can prove out the rest of what he told me you're home free, whether you did it or not." He heard the door to the room open and close behind him. "Who just came in?"

"It's Mark," Lydia's voice told him.

"My lawyer, your Mr. Jacquith, told me not to talk to the police unless I was formally charged," Sharon said.

"I'm here as a friend, not a cop, Miss Ladd," Kreevich said.

"You can trust him, Sharon," Quist said. He could hear Sharon take a deep breath and let it out in a long sigh.

"I seem to need friends," she said. She took her hands away from Quist's and he felt, suddenly, that he'd lost contact with her. But she didn't move away. "You want proof of what Bud told you," she went on. "We've tried for a long time but we never came up with anything. We believed what we suspected, but we were never able to find anything to back it up."

"You hired private detectives," Quist said.

"When we knew Bud's car had been sabotaged," Sharon said. "There wasn't any question the car had been deliberately disabled, but there was never any lead to anyone, certainly not to Leon."

"But your suspicion dated back before that."

"The Lockman family. They suspected Leon had sent a hit man to kill Billy. They had all kinds of private eyes and cops trying to prove it, but no luck. But it started me thinking, I was close to Bud then, and I told him."

"At the time, didn't it seem far-fetched to you, Sharon?" Quist asked. "What had Billy Lockman ever done to Zuck-

111

ermann? Oh, he'd barged into Zuckermann's house in Hollywood on the night of Zuckermann's wedding; Zuckermann had him thrown out on his ear and turned an attack dog loose on him. Zuckermann wins that round. Why send a paid assassin to Texas to get Billy into a row and eventually blow him away? Billy hadn't done anything to Zuckermann to make him go that far."

"You didn't know Leon," Sharon said. "Maybe no one really did. If I'd known just how far he'd go to get even I might never have pulled what I did on him. I've sometimes thought I was lucky to be alive."

"You went through a marriage ceremony and then walked out on him, having tied him up financially and made him a laughingstock in his world," Quist said. "I can imagine he might dream of—any man might dream of—getting even for that. But why Billy Lockman?"

"Poor Billy," Sharon said. "He chose the wrong moment to make a grandstand play. He heard I was marrying Leon, and he came charging up to Hollywood. Big drama for him. I think he thought of rushing up the aisle when the minister went into his 'If any man knows why these two should not be joined in wedlock let him speak now or forever hold his peace.' Billy was late for that, but he was in time to hear that I'd made my exit, laughing, without letting Leon ever lay a hand on me. Leon had him thrown out, turned his attack dog loose on him, and Billy headed back for Texas, letting everyone along the way know that I had given Leon the business. That was more than Leon's colossal ego could take. There was no way he could hurt Billy financially. The Lockmans could have bought out the Zuckermann enterprises ten times over. They have oil everywhere. Billy had no career Leon could smash. His only career was being a Lockman. So the only way to keep Billy from dining out on the shameful thing that had happened to Leon was to silence him forever."

"When you started thinking that way, weren't you afraid for yourself?" Quist asked.

"Yes and no," Sharon said. "With all Hollywood quietly laughing—and delighted by what I'd done to Leon— nothing violent could happen to me without the spotlight instantly focusing on Leon. I knew he would snipe at me forever, but I wasn't afraid of physical violence. I'd tied him up so tightly with premarital business contracts that he couldn't afford to damage me directly."

"Then Bud Tyler came into your life."

"Yes. I—I loved that man, Julian. It wasn't just a sex thing. But I couldn't stay away from an extra love life when we were separated. It's a thing I've got that I can't shake."

"Let's just say that I believe that, but I don't quite understand it," Quist said. Not even Sharon Ladd could interest him while Lydia was in his life; not Sharon or any other woman.

"Bud and I talked about Billy's murder and he came to think the way I did. Bud had friends in Texas and they did some snooping around. That's when we discovered that the Lockman family was thinking the same way. They had private detectives and the local police trying to find a lead to Leon. Nothing ever developed."

"And then?"

"I had to make a picture in England. My—my appetite for physical encounters caught up with me. I tried to play it on the level with Bud, because I cared. I told him. He—he tried to live with it. The next time I was in Hollywood, filming, and Bud had gone to Carolina to drive in a race. I—I had a thing with a big-name film star, not working in my picture, you understand." A bitter note crept into her voice. "I have never mixed business and pleasure. This time I didn't have a chance to tell Bud. Somebody beat me to it."

"An unsigned telegram to Bud in Carolina?"

113

"Yes. That's when I began to think of Leon again. It was a way for him to hurt me, a way to snipe at me. Then the terrible accident to Bud—deliberately managed. After that I really began to think Leon was after us. I hired my own private detective. Nothing."

"And when things began to go wrong for you in the *Queen Bee* rehearsals, you didn't suspect—?"

"No. And I still find it hard—"

"Bud's friends in Hollywood tell him that Zuckermann was reporting, gleefully, day by day, what was going wrong for you. Someone here was letting him know every difficulty you were having. And he broadcast to his friends, before he left Hollywood, that he was going to New York to watch you fall on your face in the first preview performances of the show."

"He was so sure you were going to fail," Kreevich said, speaking for the first time. "He had to know why to be that sure, didn't he? He had to know that you were being drugged. Since he was in Hollywood, there had to be someone here, working for him, playing games with your sleeping pills, and giving him a blow-by-blow account of how things were going."

"Oh, my God!" Sharon said in something like a whisper.

"Is there anyone in the *Queen Bee* company you know from your film work on the coast?" Kreevich asked.

Sharon hesitated. "Not from any personal contact I had with them," she said. "Marty Powell, the leading man, has made a few films, not with me, and not for Leon Zuckermann as far as I know. Sonny Wertz, the musical director, has done some film scores for Hollywood. I think Tommy Thompson, the assistant stage manager, did some work in film studios."

"Thompson tried to help you," Quist said. "He found you a doctor to go to, didn't he?"

"He's a terribly nice young guy," Sharon said. "None of

114

these people ever mentioned Leon, or working for him, or knowing him."

"Janet Lane, of course," Quist said.

"Oh, my! Dear Janet! She was the start of it all. Blacklisted, no way to get work. She finally told me how it had happened. Leon and his casting couch! It's not unheard-of in Hollywood, sex for a job. Her descriptions of Leon and the perversions he demanded of her are not for public consumption. I hated him, without ever having worked for him or laid eyes on him."

"Hated him enough to kill him?" Kreevich asked quietly.

Sharon laughed. "I suppose you could say that, like people once hated Hitler enough to kill him. I was totally impersonal. I didn't know him. But I remember telling Janet that if he ever tried his funny business on me I'd fix his wagon."

"And then he did try," Quist said.

Again the laugh, shrill and bitter. "I'm a big star, he was a big producer–director. It wasn't freakish that our professional paths would cross. He came up with a script, he needed a star, I was right for it, he asked me to come and talk to him about it."

"And you did, knowing what you knew about him from Janet Lane?" Kreevich asked.

"Just try to think straight about it for a minute, Lieutenant," Sharon said. "I was a big star. I didn't need the job, or Leon Zuckermann to help me. If it was a good script and a good deal, I would consider it. I hated him for what I knew about him but I never dreamed he'd pull his casting couch routine on me. Well, it was a good script, a marvelous script, and my agent handled the money part of the deal to everyone's satisfaction. Then Leon asked me to come out to his Hollywood place on a Sunday afternoon. He wanted to talk about other casting for the film, about my concept of certain aspects of the story. It seemed logical, not out of the ordinary for a star of my quality and a director of his stature to get together for that kind of conference."

"But Janet Lane had told you about him," Kreevich said.

"Janet was just a beginner, trying to get started, when she was subjected to Zuckermann's approach. She was unsophisticated enough to believe that she had to do what he asked if she hoped to get anywhere in Hollywood. I just didn't dream that Zuckermann would try his act on me."

"But he did?" Quist asked.

"At first it was all business. We talked about a leading man, a possible co-star. And then we talked about the script. I have to tell you, Leon was a genius when it came to story ideas and concepts. He made me see things in the script I hadn't realized were there. I was actually excited by what he suggested for me. And then—then he made his personal pitch. No way we could work together without putting sex behind us. I—I laughed at him. I didn't have to buy my way into his film. I'd already signed for it. I wouldn't have paid his price even if I was desperate for the job, which I wasn't. I had it, signed on the dotted line."

"So you laughed at him—and walked out," Kreevich said.

"That's what I meant to do, but—but he tried to force himself on me. My God, I was alone there in his house, surrounded by his people. I thought, for the first time in my life I was really going to be raped. It was like something out of a crazy comedy, him chasing me around the room. I was screaming for help that I knew nobody was going to deliver. Everybody seemed to be suddenly deaf in that house. And then—" and Sharon laughed again— "he tripped over the rug and fell flat on his fat face. I was out of there like a rocket."

"And yet later you went through the motions of marrying him," Kreevich said. "That's hard to understand if you felt the way you say you did about it."

Quist felt Sharon's hand touch his again. It was ice-cold. "How did it get to that, to a marriage?" he asked.

"I'd signed a contract for the film," Sharon said, her voice steady again. "I had to work or get in trouble with the unions, the law. Leon surprised me. The first day on the set he took me aside, apologized for what had happened, said I was so desirable, so irresistible, he'd let himself lose control. We worked efficiently and compatibly for a couple of weeks, and then he came crawling. He couldn't go on unless I'd change my mind. He wanted me more than he'd ever wanted anything in his life. When I told him to drop dead, he suggested marriage. Together we could be the queen and king of the film business. The offer of marriage should convince me that he was hopelessly in love with me. It never occurred to him that I couldn't bear the touch of his hand. His ego was so great he couldn't believe anyone could turn down such a glorious opportunity. Of course I told him, no way. The film was going to take months to make. He never let up, every day, day after day. I—I loathed him!"

"But you finally said yes," Kreevich said.

"I thought I'd teach him a lesson he'd never forget," Sharon said. "I finally said yes under certain conditions. I was to be guaranteed certain work provisions, three films whether I made them or not. And there was to be nothing between us until after we were married! He agreed. Big deal, big wedding, all of Hollywood's royalty present. There was one loathsome kiss when the minister pronounced us man and wife. I went to change out of my wedding dress into something for the honeymoon; he couldn't wait to get started. I took off, leaving him a note to let him know he'd been had, that I'd squared accounts for Janet and all the other girls he'd played games with. I left all of Hollywood laughing at him, which was exactly what I wanted."

"Pretty grim business, even for a louse!" Dan Garvey said.

"So then you married Bud Tyler," Kreevich said. "How did you get free?"

"Oh, the marriage was annulled," Sharon said. "The legal term was, I think, that it hadn't been consummated. He tried to break the money deals I'd made with him and lost."

"You didn't think he'd try to get even?" Quist asked.

"How? He couldn't hurt me professionally. He couldn't mention my name without people remembering—and laughing."

"He found a way," Quist said.

"But he's dead now," Sharon said. "He can't do me any harm."

"Maybe, after all, you did find a way to get him off your back, Miss Ladd," Kreevich said in that deadly quiet voice.

"You mean I killed him?" Sharon asked. "You can keep saying that till your head starts to spin, Lieutenant, but that won't make it so. You can never prove that I did, because I didn't!"

"If you didn't," Kreevich said, "and I don't mind telling you as I've told Julian, I don't think you did—"

"Well then—"

"You're still in danger, Miss Ladd."

"But Leon is dead!"

"Loyal troops, covering for themselves," Kreevich said. "Zuckermann was dead when Quist was shot. We haven't come up with the right leads yet."

"I want to go back to work," Sharon said. "A hundred and fifty people are waiting over at the Tempest to find out whether they can afford to buy tomorrow's lunch."

"As long as they think I plan to charge you with murder, you're safe, Miss Ladd. As long as Julian can't function, he may be safe. That's the way I want it until I can reach out and grab someone. As far as the press is concerned, you're

118

under arrest and we plan to take you before the grand jury for an indictment. As far as the press is concerned we don't see any connection between Zuckermann's murder and the shooting of Julian. That, we think—for the press—was just some psycho taking a shot at a passer-by."

"For how long do you plan to play this game, Lieutenant?" Sharon asked.

Quist could imagine the shrug of Kreevich's shoulders. "For as long as it takes to come up with an answer that makes sense. It could be an hour, a day, a week."

"You can't do this to me, Lieutenant," Sharon protested.

"I think I can—for a while, Miss Ladd. I like to sleep at night, which I couldn't do if I let you go and something happened to you. Meanwhile I have a couple of simple questions for you."

"Such as?"

"Who prescribed the Seconal capsules for you?"

"My Hollywood doctor—Dr. Gerald Markham."

"Where was the prescription filled?"

"Oh, God, Lieutenant, I've been taking those sleeping capsules for several years. A drugstore near my house in Hollywood, a chemist's in London, here in New York most recently."

"Under the law you had to have a new prescription each time. You can't just take in the empty bottle and have it refilled."

"Dr. Markham sent me a prescription each time I needed one."

"The ones you were using here in the hotel—where was that prescription filled?"

"In the drugstore down in the lobby," Sharon said.

"You carried those capsules around with you?"

"No! Why would I? I only needed them when I was ready to go to bed."

"You kept them in your room here at the hotel?"

"Yes, in the bathroom. I have to swallow them with water."

"You never noticed anything odd about the capsules?"

"No. There's no taste. You just swallow them and the capsule dissolves in your stomach."

"So there were all kinds of times, day and night—when you were at rehearsals, or dining out with friends, or involving yourself in a romance—when someone could have tampered with your capsules or substituted drugged ones for them."

"I suppose."

"Which brings me," Kreevich said, "to a question about your room key. How did you handle it?"

"I don't understand."

"Guests here in the hotel are instructed to leave their keys at the front desk when they go out," Kreevich said. "I guess that hundreds of people don't do that, and that you are one of them."

"No, I don't leave my key," Sharon said. "You may not understand how it is, Lieutenant. There are always people in the lobby sitting around, gawking. I stop to go to the desk for something and they're all over me, asking for autographs, asking me impertinent questions. I go through the lobby just as quickly as I can, trying to avoid attracting attention. I keep my key with me. They aren't going to throw me out on the street for that."

"You carry it in your purse or handbag?"

"Where else? We gals don't have pockets, Lieutenant."

Quist imagined Kreevich's acknowledging smile. "So you've been going to rehearsals every day," the detective said, "carrying your room key in your handbag. Now I suspect you don't carry that bag onstage with you when you're rehearsing."

"Of course not. I leave it in my dressing room."

"Containing money, credit cards, cosmetics—and the key?"

"Yes. But no one would think of—"

"I suspect someone thought of the key," Kreevich said. "There would have been plenty of time to take it somewhere, have a duplicate made, and return the original to your bag."

"But why?"

"To get into your room here at the hotel while you were away, play games with your sleeping pills," Kreevich said.

"And to get in after you were asleep last night," Quist said, "take your gun, go down to Twelve and murder Zuckermann, and get back into your room and replace the gun."

"So the most likely place for your key to have been lifted and copied was from your dressing room at the theater," Kreevich said. "The theater has to be our starting point. Somewhere, not too far from the theater, there must be a hardware store where a key could have been copied. Someone may remember, may be able to identify the person who brought the key in for copying. Not much we can do till shops open up in the morning."

Quist turned toward the sound of Kreevich's voice. "Unless Max Marsden can be assured Sharon can get back into his show, he's going to close up shop, Mark. Everyone connected with the company will, quite legitimately, scatter to the four winds. Goodbye, killer."

"Not till everyone connected with the show has been under my microscope," Kreevich said.

"Let me go back to work," Sharon said. "It will hold the company together."

"I can't do that, Miss Ladd, without letting the killer know that I'm looking somewhere else," Kreevich said.

"Maybe I can persuade Max to keep going," Quist said.

"Without letting the cat out of the bag?" Kreevich asked.

"The cat will be out of the bag and long gone if you don't stop playing 'Suppose,'" Garvey said.

"'Suppose'? Kreevich asked.

"I listen to you, Mark," Garvey said, impatiently, "and I

121

listen to everyone else and I can't believe what I'm hearing. Are we to 'suppose' Zuckermann hired a hit man to kill Billy Lockman because Lockman made people laugh at him? Pretty far out! He then sends his hit man to wreck Bud Tyler's car, expecting to kill him. Why? Because Tyler stole a woman he never had!"

"Or because Tyler was involved in trying to tie Zuckermann to Billy's murder," Kreevich said.

"Zuckermann has his hit man come to New York, poison Sharon's sleep medicine so she'll fail publicly. The hit man then decides to kill the goose that laid the golden eggs and frame Sharon for it. All those 'supposes' just don't add up, Mark."

"How do you see them?" Kreevich asked.

"Billy Lockman was killed in a barroom brawl, just as it was reported. No connection with Zuckermann. Bud Tyler's racing car was sabotaged by some crazy in the racing business who had a grudge against him. No connection with Zuckermann and Billy Lockman. Someone connected with *Queen Bee* has it in for Sharon and substituted drugs for her sleeping pills. No connection with Zuckermann or Billy Lockman or Bud Tyler."

"And committed a murder," Kreevich said. "That, you'll have to admit, was connected with Zuckermann! He was killed!"

"Yes—by someone who knew Sharon's habits intimately—her use of sleeping pills, that gun on her bedside table. Zuckermann never knew her that well," Garvey said.

"Which takes you where?" Kreevich asked in a strangely flat voice.

"Right to Sharon," Garvey said. "Who hated ycu and Zuckermann enough to want to kill you both, Sharon? Who knows what kind of toothpaste you use? Because he, or she, had to know you that well to know about your sleeping-pill habit and your gun."

Quist could only imagine the puzzled and frightened look that must show on Sharon's face. "Someone was reporting to Zuckermann what was going on at rehearsals," she said.

"Some gossip reporter, someone who knew how Zuckermann felt about you and hoped to get a job from him by passing along the word to him. Not necessarily anyone who dreamed of violence. Or it could have been the person we're looking for—the one who knows your intimate habits so well."

There was a moment of silence and then Sharon spoke. "Thanks, Dan," she said.

"For what?" Garvey asked.

"By making me see that I'm going to feel a lot worse than just foolish," Sharon said, "if I don't do what I can for Max Marsden and the *Queen Bee* company—by showing up, going back to work."

"You're under arrest," Kreevich said.

"The lawyer Julian got me, Mr. Jacquith, says I can get released on bail."

"And make yourself a target," Kreevich said.

"I know now why I was failing," Sharon said. To Quist, her voice seemed to come alive. "I can make them all forget what's happened! Wouldn't it help you, too, Lieutenant? You'd have the good guys and the bad guys all in one place, the Tempest Theater, locked in, you might say."

"I can't use you as bait!" Kreevich said.

"It would be easier to guard me there, out in the open, than sitting here, waiting for the wrong person to come through that door," Sharon said.

"Hard to deal with a gutsy lady, isn't it, Mark?" Garvey said. "But if you're right about the man we want not being able to run out on the company without attracting attention to himself, then Sharon's right when she says going back to work would lock him in. You can have the theater swarming

123

with cops, I can be there watching, Julian can be there—listening. It sounds foolproof to me."

Kreevich hesitated. "You really want to risk it, Miss Ladd?"

"I've got to risk it," Sharon said. "A hundred and fifty people are depending on me." Her laugh sounded a little shrill. "If something is going to happen to me, I'd rather have it be in action than just sitting here, waiting for it."

"You, Julian?" the lieutenant asked. "I know you'll insist on being there unless I make it impossible for you."

Quist felt the knots in his stomach tightening. "I don't know what I can hear that will do any good. But yes, I want to be there." He felt Sharon's cool hand cover his.

"You can hear whether I'm singing flat on the high notes," she said. "No one else will have the courage to tell me if I am."

Kreevich made up his mind. "I'll have to talk to the District Attorney. I'll let you all know as soon as I have."

On the trip back from the Beaumont's basement garage to Beekman Place, Quist was aware that he was close to exhaustion. The shock and personal anxiety brought on by his own disaster had taken more out of him than anything else he could remember. Suddenly all he wanted in the world was to crawl into his own bed and pray for oblivion.

He rode in the back seat of the special police car with Lydia; Garvey was up front with the plainclothes driver. As the car approached the Beekman Place apartment house it slowed down.

"What the hell!" the driver said.

Quist opened his eyes—and saw nothing. "What is it?"

"Three or four police cars just outside your building," the driver said. "Here comes one of the cops."

"What's up?" the driver asked.

"Mugging," a strange voice outside the car answered. "Some dame walking along, guy evidently came up behind her, snatched her handbag, leaving no I.D. Slugged her in the back of the head with what they call a blunt instrument when they don't know what it is."

"Hurt bad?"

The outside voice was angry. "If being dead is bad then it's bad," he said. "There are so many crazy hopped-up bastards on the streets these nights . . . !"

"I've got a blind man here. Can I drive him up to the door?"

"Sure, why not?"

The car moved a few yards farther on and stopped. Lydia and Garvey walked on each side of Quist across the sidewalk and into the lobby of the building. The night doorman asked Quist if he was all right.

"Thanks, Eddie. I guess the phrase is 'right as can be expected.' You see what happened out there?"

"No, sir. I was inside, heard a scream, ran out. This dame was lying on the sidewalk, all blood. I called the cops."

"You didn't see the mugger?"

"Didn't see anyone. He just slugged her, grabbed her bag, and took off, I guess. Getting so it isn't safe to be out after dark these days."

The three friends went up in the elevator to Quist's apartment.

"Can I fix you something, Julian?" Lydia asked. "Coffee? A sandwich?"

"All I want, luv, is to climb into the sack and dive off," Quist said. "Thanks, Dan, for standing by. When we hear from Kreevich I'll let you know."

"I'm not going anywhere," Garvey said. "You and Lydia get some rest. I'll take over the living-room couch—just in case."

125

"That's not necessary, Dan. There's a cop downstairs, the doorman."

"If you don't mind, I'd like to make certain for myself," Garvey said.

Lydia guided Quist to their second-floor bedroom. Minutes later he was gratefully in bed, and minutes after that Lydia slipped in beside him. He supposed the lights were off. For him the whole world was dark. He felt her head against his shoulder as he began to drift away.

The telephone rang.

"For God's sake take that thing off the hook," Quist muttered.

Garvey had evidently picked up on the second ring downstairs.

"Dan will turn whoever it is off," Lydia said.

Quist began to drift away again.

There was a knock on the bedroom door. "Sorry to do this to you," Garvey said. His voice sounded harsh.

"Can't it wait till morning?" Lydia asked.

"I thought not," Garvey said. "They've identified the woman who was mugged outside this building."

Quist felt himself swimming to the surface again. "It's important?" he heard himself ask.

"It was Janet Lane," Garvey said. "D.O.A.—dead on arrival at the hospital. It seems there was some kind of blood-type information pinned inside her dress. They were able to trace it and identify her."

"Oh, my God," Lydia said.

"You have to guess she was coming here to see you, Julian," Garvey said.

PART THREE

1 "That was Kreevich on the telephone," Garvey said. "He wants you and Lydia out of this room, out of this apartment, just as fast as you can make it."

"Why?" Quist managed, out of the darkness that insisted on dragging him back down.

"Janet Lane was obviously coming here to see you," Garvey said. "She wouldn't have been sightseeing on Beekman Place at eleven o'clock at night."

"She must have thought Julian was in the hospital," Lydia said. "Why would she come here?"

"Bud Tyler found out he wasn't in the hospital. Janet Lane evidently had a way of finding out, too. Get moving."

Quist lay back on his pillow. Anything was better than having to move. "Why?" he repeated.

"There are cops on the way," Garvey said. "Just cover yourself with a bathrobe, anything, and move! Even if we have to sit out in the hall!"

"You're not making sense, Dan."

"It's Mark Kreevich who's making sense," Garvey said. "Janet Lane came here to see you. She spotted someone coming out of the building she knew. She had to be silenced."

"One word again, Dan—why?"

129

"If this psycho, whoever he is, managed to get into your apartment, there may be a booby trap set up here ready to blow us all to hell and gone."

"How could anyone possibly have gotten in here, Dan?" Lydia asked. "There was the doorman, the lobby attendant, a cop on duty."

"And they all knew there was no one here—all gone to the Beaumont in a police car. They relaxed! Someone went somewhere for a short beer! This crazy has a genius for getting in places. He got into Sharon's suite in the well-guarded Beaumont, didn't he? So get moving. Just throw something around you. Don't open doors or drawers. It might trigger something."

"You know something, Dan? I just don't care," Quist said. Anything not to have to move from this place of rest.

"Then I'll carry you!" Garvey said.

Lydia hadn't waited for arguments, or to get Julian a robe. She slipped into her own dressing gown, which had been on a chair beside the bed. She pulled down the covers off Quist and Garvey yanked his friend up into a sitting position. Lydia took a blanket off the bed and wrapped it around Quist's pajamaed shoulders.

"You've got to try, Julian," she said.

Against his will, Quist was surfacing again. He swung his legs over the side of the bed and felt Garvey's strong arm lifting him to his feet. They made it down the stairs, across the living room, and to the front door. Someone was banging on the door. It was the special cop assigned to guard Quist.

"The building manager's office at the lobby level," he said. "They've got it ready for you."

"Ready for what?" Quist asked.

"The bomb squad guys are on their way to go over your place, Mr. Quist. Lieutenant Kreevich's orders."

They headed toward the waiting elevator.

"There are two uniformed cops in the car, Julian," Lydia said.

"This all seems pretty far-fetched," Quist heard himself say. But he walked now, without Garvey's support, his hand on Lydia's arm. The elevator sank down to the lobby level.

"I don't know how anybody could have got up there, Mr. Quist." Quist recognized the lobby attendant's voice. "Of course, we knew you weren't up there. He could have gone up with other people. We could have thought he was part of a party."

"Just get me out of sight, will you, Eddie?" Quist said. He felt helpless and naked.

He had never been in the building manager's office. He had no idea what it looked like. He was suddenly standing in an unknown space, a humming sound in his ears.

"What's that noise?" he asked.

"Air conditioning. There aren't any windows in this room," Garvey said. "Here's a chair. Sit down."

It was like the hospital, a zero. Quist had no idea whether it was big or small. He'd been able to visualize the hospital room at the Beaumont where Sharon was held. He'd been there when he could see. His own apartment he could have managed in the dark when he could see. But this!

"It's a small room, Julian," Lydia said. She, bless her, understood. "A big flat-topped desk, four chairs, a row of metal filing cabinets. There are some photographs on the walls, famous tenants I suspect." She laughed softly. "Believe it or not, there's one of you, Julian! It was taken here in the lobby when you were interviewed by reporters here a couple of years ago. A party you were giving for Ian McCloud. You remember? It's you and Ian with big grins on your faces."

"I managed to sneak a bottle of Jack Daniels off the bar

upstairs before we left," Garvey said. "I think there's a john off to the rear here. We may get lucky and find some paper cups. It's been too long between drinks." His voice faded away on that last and then came back strong. "God is with us. Paper cups, water. Here, Julian. Take a swig of this and see what it will do for you."

The whiskey was warm and comforting. Quist found himself beginning to believe that he just might make it. The door opened behind him and he turned, not that it mattered.

"It's Mark, Julian," Lydia said.

"Thank God you're down here safe," Kreevich said.

"What do you expect to find upstairs, Mark?" Quist asked.

"Nothing, I hope," Kreevich said. "I couldn't take the chance, though."

"How did you get into the act?" Garvey asked.

"Piece of luck," Kreevich said. "The street cops took the mugger's victim to the hospital. D.O.A. No identification. Her handbag was gone. But some people who have rare blood types carry that information in case of accident. This woman had a tag pinned inside her dress. It gave the blood type, the name of a Beverly Hills hospital, and an identification number. They called the hospital, got the name—Janet Lane. The name's been in the papers and on radio and TV during the day—part of the Sharon Ladd story. Someone had the brains to call me."

"So what's with bomb squads?" Garvey said.

"Another one of your games of 'suppose,'" Kreevich said. He sounded less than cheerful. "Janet Lane found out that Julian wasn't at the hospital, came here to see him. She saw something or someone that would have made her dangerous and the killer polished her off, taking her handbag to make it look like an ordinary street mugging."

"So why does that make you suspect a bomb?" Garvey said.

132

"It's become a popular way to eliminate people—all around the world," Kreevich said. "You plant a time bomb and you can be in the next county before it goes off, perfectly alibied. If someone did booby-trap your apartment, Julian, and Janet Lane, by an unfortunate accident, saw him coming out of this building, that would account for what happened to her."

"How would she know a mad bomber when she saw one?" Garvey asked.

"I don't know—yet," Kreevich said.

"There's a question I'd like to ask," Quist said. It was difficult for him to concentrate. All he wanted to do was lean back and slip away.

"Shoot," Kreevich said.

"I know how Bud Tyler found out I'd left the hospital, a friendly nurse. How did Janet Lane know?"

"Pressure of the press and TV people may have broken down our fences at the hospital," Kreevich said.

"So why didn't Janet Lane phone me to discover if I could see her instead of just coming unannounced?"

"You weren't here," Kreevich said. "She could have phoned and gotten no answer. She could have guessed you weren't answering the phone and decided to come directly to you."

"What could have been so important?" Garvey asked.

"Maybe she came up with the crank letter Julian thought might turn up," Kreevich said. "Maybe she got some kind of a tip from some friend of hers or Sharon's in Hollywood. Maybe she was just concerned and wanted to see for herself that Julian was all right."

"Maybe, maybe, maybe," Garvey said.

"So give us time, Dan," the detective said. "If the cupboard's bare upstairs then we can breathe a little easier."

"Does Sharon know what's happened?" Quist asked. "Janet was a close friend."

"She doesn't know from me," Kreevich said, "and we

133

haven't released Janet's identity to the reporters. It won't be on the radio or TV just yet."

"She might know someone who had it in for Janet," Quist said.

That angry note was back in Garvey's voice. "You going to revive the idea that Zuckermann is still giving orders from the morgue?"

Quist suddenly realized that he had done what he had dreamed of doing—just leaned back in his chair and gone to sleep. Someone had him by the shoulder and was shaking him gently. It was Lydia.

"Julian!"

"I never thought I'd hope you'd leave me alone," Quist muttered.

"We can go back upstairs now," Lydia said.

"How long have I been asleep?"

"A couple of hours."

"The cupboard was bare, then?"

Lydia's voice sounded tense. "No, it wasn't."

Quist sat up very straight. "They found something?"

"In the medicine cabinet in your bathroom," Lydia said. "If you'd stopped last night to brush your teeth, or tried to shave in the morning—"

"A bomb?"

"According to Mark, enough to blow you and most of the top floor of the duplex to pieces. The police have gone over the whole place up there for fingerprints. So far, nothing. Julian, hadn't we better go away somewhere, hide out, until this thing is all over?"

"And wait to be hit when everything has quieted down? No, ma'am! Let's get back up there and see what's cooking."

When they got back up to the apartment the sergeant in

charge of the bomb squad told Quist what they'd found. A small but deadly bomb had been placed in the medicine cabinet over the wash basin in Quist's bathroom. If he had opened the mirror-covered door of the cabinet, it would have triggered an explosion that would almost certainly have had fatal consequences.

As Quist listened he was aware that Garvey wasn't with them, that Kreevich wasn't there. He found himself hanging on to Lydia, his only contact with anything familiar.

"You know how someone got in here?" he heard himself ask. "The door wasn't forced or smashed, was it? I can't see, you know, but my friend Garvey or Miss Morton would have noticed."

"A piece of bad luck for you, good luck for the bomber," the police officer said. "The service area. You put your trash, garbage, out there for the building maintenance people to pick up. Door opens out of your kitchen, right? Whoever put your last trash bags out there didn't close the door tightly when they came back in. We think the man just found that door open and walked in."

"I—I'm responsible," Lydia said, her voice shaky.

"Don't lose sleep over it," the policeman said. "There was nobody in the apartment. Our man could have picked the lock, forced the door, if he'd had to."

"Fingerprints?" Quist asked.

"There are fingerprints all over the place, particularly in that bathroom. Yours, I suspect, and Miss Morton's. The same prints we found in the bathroom are down here in the kitchen, in that little service bar of yours. We'll check them out, but I think they have to be yours, Mr. Quist's and Miss Morton's in the kitchen and in the second bathroom upstairs."

"That doesn't speak too well for our cleaning woman," Lydia said. "She was here yesterday morning."

"You don't stop to think how many places you touch in

135

the place where you live in a short time," the policeman said. "Since there seems to be just those two sets of prints everywhere, we think the man we're after must have been wearing some kind of gloves."

"Materials in the bomb lead you anywhere?" Quist asked.

"Could have come from a thousand places," the policeman said. "Everything wiped clean before it was put in place."

"Dead end?"

"So far, I'm afraid so," the policeman said.

Almost three o'clock in the morning, Lydia told Quist. Hell, he couldn't read his own watch! She didn't know where Dan or Kreevich had gone. As soon as the word had come that the bomb had been found, they'd both taken off. Garvey had said something about back-checking on the unhappy Janet Lane. Kreevich was trying to find out how the bomber had got past the security that had been set up in the building.

"There's no reason why you can't go back to the upstairs quarters," the policeman said. "Lieutenant Kreevich has an army patrolling the halls, the service area, the whole building from the roof to the basement. There'll be a couple of cops down here in your living room."

"I—I never thought I would want to sleep when someone was out to get me," Quist said. "But this has been quite a day."

"Get your sleep," the policeman said. "There's nothing you can do to help."

Quist wondered, with a kind of sick despair, if he'd be hearing that phrase forever—"nothing you can do to help." *Because you're blind!*

Lydia guided him back upstairs to the bedroom.

"I almost feel that I don't dare touch anything," she said.

"They'll have been over every inch of the place," Quist

136

said. "Please don't leave me, luv. If Dan or Mark come up with anything, they'll wake us."

"I won't leave you, Julian, ever," Lydia said. "I promise."

For just a moment he held her close. "I'm going to have to learn to function by myself," he said. "But I need a little time."

"Of course, my darling. The bed's just there to your right. Let me tuck you in."

It didn't seem possible, but sleep came almost at once, even before Lydia could join him in the king-size bed. It must have been hours and hours, he thought, as he felt himself stirring.

He opened his eyes. The sun was streaming through the bedroom windows. For just a second or two he didn't realize what had happened. He turned his head, and there was Lydia sleeping quietly beside him, her red-brown hair spread out on the pillow. Dear God, *he could see!*

He opened his mouth to shout, and instead he turned, slipped an arm under Lydia, and pressed his cheek against hers.

"You want something, Julian?" she whispered, still half asleep.

"You are, my darling, as the saying goes, a sight for sore eyes," he said. "You are the most beautiful thing I ever saw in all my life."

"You're remembering something that isn't so," she said. Then she opened her eyes. "Julian!"

"I can see, I can see, *I can see!*" He held her close for an instant, then bounded out of bed and went to the windows. "The most beautiful city in the world! Oh, my God, Lydia!"

"When, Julian?"

"I woke up, opened my eyes, and someone had turned on the light switch!"

"Oh Julian, my darling! Dr. Jorgensen said it could happen like that. We must let Dan know, Mark know."

He came back from the windows and sat down on the edge of the bed beside her. "Maybe there is something I can do now to help." He took her hands in his. "Don't spread the word yet, luv. Dan and Mark, of course. But it just may be that being blind—and able to see—could be useful."

Quist shaved in front of the mirror that could have been a deathtrap some hours ago. Except for the strip of hair shaved from the right side of his head, he looked pretty normal, he thought. He was able to think now without the awful panic that had engulfed him for almost a whole day. Somewhere, probably at the Tempest Theater, a psychotic monster was waiting to hear the news that he'd been blown to pieces. There might be some reaction he could see when he walked in there in one piece.

He dressed, and when someone knocked on the bedroom door, he went to the bedside table, picked up the dark glasses he'd worn yesterday and put them on.

"Come in," he called out.

It was Kreevich. He looked beat, like a man who'd been put through a cement mixer. "I see you managed to shave and dress," the detective said. "You're a fast learner." Obviously Lydia hadn't told him.

"I'd also like to say," Quist said. "that that's a hell of a looking necktie you're wearing."

Kreevich stopped dead in his tracks in the doorway. "You gave it to me last Christmas," he said. "Julian—?"

"I can see, Mark! I can see just as well as I ever did."

Kreevich took a quick step forward and for a moment the two friends found themselves in a bear hug.

"Oh, Julian, how great!" Kreevich said, pushing back and looking at his friend. "I've been so damn worried about you."

"I woke up and there it was, just as though nothing had ever happened."

138

"Why the glasses?" Kreevich asked.

"I want to talk to you about that, but first you came here to tell me something."

A little nerve twitched on Kreevich's cheek. "I came to tell you that there's nothing to tell," he said. "Lydia was getting you breakfast, said you were up. She didn't tell me there'd been a miracle."

"I wanted to talk to you about it. But you don't have anything?"

Kreevich shrugged. My God, Quist thought, he could see! He could see his friend's weariness and distress. He couldn't have had any sleep at all in the last twenty-four hours. His eyes were red-rimmed, and there was a dark shadow of beard on his unshaven face. The harsh, flat voice wouldn't have told Quist much last night, except that his friend was a cop at work. Now he could see the ravages of hours of unremitting—and unrewarding—work.

"We're still loaded with Dan's 'supposes,'" Kreevich said, bitterness there. "People on the floor below you, name of Weatherby. You know them?"

"Just a name on the bulletin board in the lobby," Quist said. "Done a couple of hellos on the elevator. Young couple with a poodle dog."

"Young Mr. Weatherby, Paul Weatherby, got a job promotion yesterday," Kreevich said. "He threw a party at a fancy bar down the street, a dinner party. Maybe a dozen people."

"Must have been a good promotion," Quist said. "A dozen people at today's prices . . ."

"After dinner they came back here, all of them, to carry on the celebration in the Weatherbys' apartment. A dozen people swarmed in off the sidewalk together. The restaurant was only a couple of blocks away, so they walked. I remembered someone said something about 'part of a party.' It was the only sort of gang entrance to the building during the evening. The cop I had down there, the build-

139

ing attendants, were assured by Weatherby that they were all his friends. I went to question Weatherby. Somebody on one of the elevators—they had to use two to get that crowd upstairs—remembered that there was someone on the elevator who wasn't one of them. They didn't think anything of it. They didn't know there was anything wrong in the building, that there was anything wrong about a stranger being on the same elevator with them."

"Description?"

Kreevich shook his head. "A fair-haired guy in a blue suit, a dark-haired guy in a gray suit! Everybody was a little drunk, laughing, joking."

"So?"

"If this man in the blue–gray suit with the fair–dark hair had come in alone ahead of the Weatherby mob, he'd have been questioned by the cop on duty, or the building attendant. Or at least identified by the building people as someone who belonged here. But he seems to have come in off the street, mingling in the Weatherby crowd. 'These are all my friends,' Weatherby told the cop on duty. Weatherby doesn't remember this guy, he wasn't on the car Weatherby took up. If he belonged here, I think the building attendant would have seen him, recognized him. I have the slim hope that he was our man, and that the two people who remember him may be able to pick him out from the people at the Tempest this morning."

"You think the guy you're after may still be there?"

Kreevich indulged again in the bitter little shrug of his shoulders. "We've only got two places," he said. "The theater and the hotel? Until we know more there's no other place to look."

"Except this building, this neighborhood," Quist said.

"Where we look for a young man with fair–dark hair and a blue–gray suit. I'm prepared to narrow our search to one place," Kreevich said. "The Tempest Theater."

"You're going to let Sharon Ladd go there?"

Kreevich nodded. "And you, if you're willing. You and Sharon appear to be this bastard's primary targets, and we have a better chance of protecting you if you're both in the same place."

"Should I paint a target on the back of my jacket?" Quist asked, with a tight smile.

"It's already there," Kreevich said. "He's missed you twice now. How long can your luck hold out?"

"Why the hell am I so important to him?" Quist asked.

"More guesses," Kreevich said. "You're trying to divert my attention from Sharon Ladd. I'm supposed to send her up for life. And if he's as crazy as I think he is, he won't forgive you for trying to screw up his diabolical little plan for Sharon."

"So you present us to him—at the Tempest?"

"Surrounded by a small army of cops," Kreevich said, "we keep the show rehearsing because we think he can't walk away without calling attention to himself."

"I'm willing," Quist said. "In fact I'm eager. I'd rather go after him than wait for him to come after me."

"Good man," Kreevich said. "So have your breakfast coffee and let's get moving."

"You asked about these glasses," Quist said.

"Trying to surprise me, I suppose," Kreevich said.

"Something else, Mark. It occurred to me that if no one knows that I've recovered my sight, this creep might do something or show something that would give him away."

Kreevich's tired eyes widened. "It's an idea."

"You, Lydia, and Dan Garvey, when I catch up with him, would be the only ones who know I can see. No cops, no one at the Tempest, no one else. It might invite a move from this character if he thought he was safe in my presence."

"I'll buy it," Kreevich said.

2 Nine-thirty in the morning.

There was a squad of cops outside the Tempest Theater, keeping a reluctant crowd moving. Quist and Lydia arrived at the front entrance in a police car and walked under the marquee and into the theater. The "blind" Quist was guided by Lydia through the back of the house and up the stairs to Max Marsden's office.

The clan was gathered, Kreevich, Sharon Ladd—looking gorgeous—Marsden, Larry Shields and three other men Quist didn't know. It was more like a wake than a rehearsal. Quist tried to remember what they knew and what they didn't know. They didn't know that he could see, they knew that Janet Lane was dead, they didn't know that a bomb had been set in Quist's apartment—unless one of them was the bomber.

Only Sharon Ladd had seen Quist since he'd been shot at and blinded the day before. There were muttered expressions of sympathy. The three men Quist didn't know were introduced—Sonny Wertz, the musical director, a short, stocky little man with wire-rimmed glasses, George Hendrix, the author of the novel on which *Queen Bee* was based, a white-haired man in his early sixties, and Peter Romulus, the obviously homosexual choreographer, waved

142

hair worn long. None of them could be the fair–dark young man in the blue–gray suit who'd been in the Weatherby party the night before.

"Julian, I'm sorry I got you into this mess," Max Marsden said. "They tell me the doctors say you're going to come out of it sooner or later."

"They hope and I hope," Quist said.

"I don't know why the lieutenant wants you here, or any of us here for that matter," Marsden said. "This ball game is over."

"No!" Sharon Ladd said. "We're going on with it, Max, we're going to have a hit, we're going to be able to celebrate."

"After how many funerals?" Marsden asked, in a dull voice.

"I've explained to Marsden that he has to keep going so that the man we're looking for doesn't have an excuse to walk out on us," Kreevich said.

"And you're inviting him to have a second chance at Sharon and Julian by having them here where he can get at them," Marsden said.

"They're safer here than anywhere else," Kreevich said.

"It's not going to be easy to rehearse a show with everyone looking back over his shoulder," Larry Shields said.

"You can always leave Max looking back over his shoulder at eight or ten million bucks," Quist said.

"I'd like to believe we can go on," Larry Shields said. This big, tall, blond man couldn't be the Weatherbys' uninvited guest, Quist thought. No one could be vague about describing him. "But we've got over a hundred and fifty people here who are more or less in shock," Shields went on. "The murder of Zuckermann, the possibility that Sharon may have done it. Oh, I know that may not be so, Sharon, and that if it is someone set you up. Then there's the attack on Quist, and now the brutal mugging of Janet

143

Lane. Nobody is going to fall back into the world of make-believe too easily. The realities are too rough."

"Not exactly magic time," Peter Romulus, the campy choreographer, said.

"Maybe, in a few days . . . ?" Shields suggested.

"The theater is a world of superstitions," Max Marsden said in a tired voice. "Have one piece of bad luck and you get convinced you're going to have more and more, right down to the end of things."

"Let me put it on the line for all of you," Kreevich said. "Take a few days off and our man can be gone. I don't have the manpower to put a tail on every one of a hundred and fifty people."

"But you've said if he goes, he'll give himself away," Marsden said.

"But we could lose him," Kreevich said. "If this psycho is determined to destroy Miss Ladd, he'll be back later, with no way for us to guess when or where he'll come from. If he's here, working, he'll have to do whatever he does with dozens of us watching him."

Including, Quist thought, a blind man who can see.

"People have to go home at night," Marsden said. "We can't work round the clock."

"Miss Ladd and Julian Quist will be safe," Kreevich said. "I can protect them."

"You didn't do so well protecting Janet, did you, Lieutenant?" Peter Romulus said. "You didn't know this kook would be after her, did you? Maybe he's got some-body else in mind you don't know about." The sardonic sound of the man's voice didn't make his suggestion seem any less real.

Lydia had gone through the motions of leading Quist to a chair where he sat, watching from behind his dark lenses. "It would be interesting to know why Janet thought she'd find me at home," he said. "I was supposed to be in the

144

hospital. Was she close to anyone in the company, someone she might have confided in?"

"Me," Sharon said, "only she didn't."

"I've heard you mention an assistant stage manager who was assigned to help you, Sharon," Quist said. "Was his name Thompson? He must have talked with Janet, hoping to get some clue from her as to what was bothering you."

"Tommy Thompson," Sharon said. "He suggested that I go to see a doctor he knew. I suppose he and Janet did talk together. As a matter of fact, she went with us to see Dr. Wiseman. She might have talked to him."

"It might help if he could tell us if she mentioned trying to get to me," Quist said.

"I'll send for him," Marsden said, and reached for the phone on his desk.

"It seems to me there are things you can do today, Larry, that wouldn't involve sensitive acting," Quist said to the director. "I seem to have heard about mechanical things, the flying routines."

"God knows our clubfooted chorus could stand some drilling on the dance routines," Peter Romulus said.

"The orchestra needs the work," Sonny Wertz, the musical director, said. "The first-act climax is a shambles so far."

"And I can do my thing in a thunderstorm, the way I feel right now," Sharon Ladd said. "This isn't Shakespeare, you know."

"So you can all work at bits and pieces of the show," Kreevich said. "While that's going on, we can interrogate the people who aren't involved at the moment. Before the end of the rehearsal period we may come up with something."

"And if you don't?" Marsden asked. He'd put down his phone. "Thompson's on his way up here."

"If we don't, we start over again tomorrow."

"And a few more thousand dollars go down the drain,"

Peter Romulus said. The acid sound of his voice was getting on everyone's nerves.

"If Max says so, I'm ready to go," Larry Shields said.

"I don't have much choice, do I?" Marsden said.

Shields, Romulus, Wertz, and Hendrix left the office together, leaving Quist and Lydia with Marsden, Kreevich, and Sharon.

"Can you people find out from this Thompson guy what he knows?" Kreevich asked. "I'd like to make sure everything is covered downstairs. I need to set up a place where we can talk to people."

"My dressing room," Sharon suggested. "Poor Max spent a fortune making it habitable. I'm sure we won't be bothering with costumes and makeup today."

Quist told himself he would stay to talk to Thompson and then go down to where the action was. He watched Kreevich go and realized that he didn't feel quite as secure as he had with his detective friend present. He glanced at Lydia. She could be in danger, too, because someone knew that she was his whole life. If anything happened to her, there would be more than one psycho loose on the town!

Young Mr. Thompson was not unexpected. Sharon, somewhere along the way, had described him as "a really nice guy." He was tallish, a trim figure, blond hair worn in a crew cut. He was wearing blue jeans and a blue work shirt, with a package of cigarettes peeping out of the shirt pocket, and carrying a clipboard.

"You wanted me, Mr. Marsden," he said as he came into the office. Then he spotted Sharon, who had moved over by the window. "Sharon! I heard you were coming but I didn't know you were here." He hurried to her and gave her a brotherly kiss on the cheek. "I tried to get in to see you at the hotel, but they wouldn't let me. My God, you look great!"

Sharon smiled at him. "You know George Burns's

146

definition of the three ages of man, Tommy? 'Youth, middle age, and you look great.' I'm not there yet, Tommy boy. This is Julian Quist, and Miss Morton."

Thompson turned. He smiled at Lydia and focused on Quist. "You've really had it bad, Mr. Quist. I'm glad to see you're up and around."

Quist touched the dark glasses he was wearing. "A little handicapped at the moment," he said.

"Some kind of nut on the loose," Thompson said. "Sharon, then you, then poor, harmless Janet. It's just not believable."

"It's Janet we wanted to talk to you about, Tommy," Sharon said.

"I couldn't believe it when I heard it on the radio this morning," Thompson said. "Poor lady mugged by some common street crook. Near where you live, I understand, Mr. Quist."

"Right outside the building," Quist said. "It makes us think she was on the way to see me."

"Oh, brother!"

"I was supposed to be in the hospital," Quist said. "I was moved out and taken home to keep the press off my back. It's important for us to know how Janet knew that. We thought she might have talked to you."

"No! I mean—when we heard you'd been shot yesterday, she was telling everyone she'd just been talking to you. She was going through Sharon's mail, and moments after you'd left her—"

"She didn't tell you later that I'd been taken home and that she was going to try to see me?"

"No. I don't think I saw her after the middle of the day. Things were pretty hectic around here, cops, everybody being searched for a gun. They spent a lot of time with Janet because you'd just spent some time with her. But I didn't talk to her after that." Thompson shook his head,

147

looking genuinely puzzled. "Why would she come to see you? Of course, she knew you, could have been concerned about you."

"She could have found something in Sharon's mail," Quist said. "Sharon was in the Beaumont's hospital unit, suspected of Zuckermann's murder. I'd told Janet that I didn't go along with the police. If she'd come onto something she thought would help me help Sharon—"

"She'd have let you run over her with a truck if she thought it would help Sharon." Thompson shook his head. "She loved you an awful lot, Missy."

"I know," Sharon said, her voice suddenly unsteady. "So they can run over me with a truck if it will help get the bastard who killed her."

Thompson turned back to Quist. "I wish I knew how I could help," he said. He fished a cigarette out of the pack in his shirt pocket. "The whole damn series of things is pretty dizzy-making, you know, Mr. Quist?"

"I know," Quist said. He reached up again to touch his dark glasses. "It's not comfortable to think that the man we're after is working right here in the theater, shoulder to shoulder with you."

"You think that!"

"I think it, Lieutenant Kreevich thinks it. That's why you're back in rehearsal, so he won't be able to duck out on us without letting us know who he is."

"Brother!" Thompson said. His surprise seemed genuine.

"Janet must have talked to you a lot about Sharon when Max asked you for special help with her."

"For which I'll always be grateful, Tommy," Sharon said.

"We couldn't understand what was knocking you off the rails, Missy," Thompson said. "Now we hear someone substituted drugs for your regular sleeping pills. God!"

"It resulted in the perfect frame," Quist said. "Did Janet

148

talk to you at all about Zuckermann? She hated him, you know."

"But try to frame Sharon for his murder? Never!" Thompson said.

"I wasn't suggesting that," Quist said. "What I'm asking is, did Janet talk to you about Zuckermann after the news broke that he'd been murdered? Did she mention anyone in the company who might have worked for him, known him, hated him for some reason?"

"Not Janet," Thompson said, "but of course everyone was talking about him yesterday morning. Bits and pieces, Peter Romulus, our choreographer, made a film with him. You know Peter? He has something sour to say about everyone in the world. I heard him say Zuckermann had been inviting some kind of violence for years."

"And ready to frame Sharon in the process?" Quist asked. "We have to try to keep what facts we have in order. Whoever was trying to put Sharon out of business had been working at it since rehearsals began—three weeks ago. It didn't just happen on the spur of the moment. Bud Tyler, Sharon's ex-husband, says Zuckermann was boasting in Hollywood that he had a day-to-day report on how Sharon was messing up. He was going to come East to see her fail. But nobody could have arranged their meeting in the Beaumont lobby. That was pure coincidence." Quist glanced at Sharon. She was actually blushing. "Sharon was supposed to be having dinner with Lydia and me, changed her mind at the last minute, went back to the hotel and stumbled into Zuckermann. The man we're looking for must have been there, seen what happened, and used it as a way to do both Zuckermann and Sharon in for keeps."

"The jerk was a fast thinker," Thompson said. "There are a couple of others here who knew Zuckermann. Sonny Wertz, our musical director, scored a film for him once. He doesn't remember him with pleasure. One of the stage

149

carpenters, Dick Willis, worked on a set for Zuckermann, but he says he had no contact with him. I have to tell you, Mr. Quist, I've never heard anyone say anything good about Leon Zuckermann."

"But what we saw in the movie houses," Sharon said, "was close to genius."

"You don't have to be a sweetheart to be good at your job," Thompson said.

"But Tyler thinks Zuckermann was behind the drugging of Sharon," Quist said.

Thompson glanced at Sharon. "I guess he had reason to hate you, didn't he, Missy?"

"I guess."

"If that's how it was," Quist said, "then Zuckermann had to have someone working for him, because he himself was in Hollywood until day before yesterday. That someone is here in the company; that someone had access to Sharon's dressing room, to her handbag and her hotel key, eventually to her suite at the Beaumont, her sleeping pills, and finally her gun."

"Maybe not working for Zuckermann at all, just for himself," Max Marsden said from where he was slumped in his chair.

"Let's go back to Janet Lane for a moment," Quist said. "She was on her way to my apartment to see me. How did she know I was there? I was supposed to be at the hospital."

"I—I've been thinking about that, Julian," Lydia said. "Bud Tyler knew you were at home, from a nurse who took care of him when he was a patient at St. Clare's. Were he and Janet friends, Miss Ladd? Could he have told her where to find Julian?"

"Why yes, they were friends," Sharon said. "I mean, for the year that I was married to Bud, Janet was working for me, had been for several years. Their paths crossed all the

150

time. I think they got along well, nothing special, but friendly."

Quist almost reached for Marsden's telephone, but checked himself in time. He wasn't supposed to be able to see. He took his wallet out of his inside jacket pocket and held it out in the direction of Lydia.

"I have his address and phone number written down on something in this," he said. "You remember I went to see him before all this exploded. I was trying to find out about your drinking habits, Sharon. See if you can get Bud on the phone, Lydia."

Lydia found the number, dialed it, and listened to the sound of the ringing that wasn't answered. "Not there," she said as she put down the phone.

"There are so damned many coincidences, Mr. Quist," Thompson said. "Is it possible she wasn't looking for you at all? I mean, been to see someone in that part of town and just happened to be passing your building?"

"And was hit by some unconnected street mugger?" Quist asked. "That's a coincidence I just can't buy." Kreevich wanted it kept secret for the moment or he would have mentioned the bomb planted in his medicine cabinet. There was no question in his mind that Janet Lane had come to Beekman Place to find him, that she'd seen someone she knew leaving the building, and been killed to keep her from reporting to the police, who she'd seen—after the bomb had blown him into the next world. She'd seen someone she knew who was almost certainly now somewhere in this theater.

"I wish I could be more help," Thompson said. "If Larry's starting a rehearsal I should be down there, backstage, doing my job. There's enough confusion without his having to have someone stand in for me."

"Keep your eyes and ears open," Quist said.

"I'd better get down there, too," Sharon said. She

151

hesitated. "Should I let the lieutenant know that you're up here alone, Julian?"

"I'm not alone," Quist said. "There's Lydia and Max."

"I meant, without a cop to protect you," Sharon said. "If this creature is waiting for a chance to get at you . . . ?"

"You're the one who needs guarding," Quist said.

"I'll stay with her till the cops can take over," Thompson said.

Quist watched them open the office door to leave. They stopped in the doorway. Sharon turned back, giving Quist a nervous little laugh. "It seems the lieutenant hasn't forgotten us," she said.

A uniformed cop appeared in the doorway. "We'll take Miss Ladd back down to the stage," the man said. "There's an officer out here in the hall if you need anything, Mr. Quist."

"What I need," Quist said, "are answers."

"Julian, this isn't going to work, you know," Max Marsden said when he and Quist and Lydia were alone in the office. "It will take days for the police to question everyone in this company. The first preview performance is scheduled for Monday. We're going to have to cancel it because a company of frightened people aren't going to be able to give a decent public performance. I'm not going to be able to raise fresh money if we have to keep delaying. Nobody's going to take a chance on putting up new financing. Audiences will stay away in droves, knowing there may be a killer in the theater with them."

"Just fasten your seat belt, Max," Quist said. "We may get lucky before it's too late."

Marsden's laugh was hollow. "Has it occurred to you, Julian, that if the only way this madman can get away without drawing attention to himself is to close the show—that if I'm not around, it will close?"

"You scared, Max?"

"Out of my wits," the old man said, and slumped deeper into his chair. "You grow old telling yourself you're not afraid of dying, and then when you're threatened with it, your blood turns to ice water."

"Kreevich isn't going to let anything happen to anyone," Quist said.

"He hasn't done too well so far, has he?" Marsden said. "Sharon, Zuckermann, you, Janet. Someone else won't make him look much worse, will it?"

"Kreevich is a topflight cop, Max," Quist said. "One of the headaches of his business is that he doesn't get called onto the scene until after a crime has been committed and the investigation is in motion. Yesterday he had every reason to believe Sharon had killed Zuckermann; it had been carefully set up for him to buy that. He knows better now, he knows where his man is, and he isn't going to let him strike again. But I'll tell him what you're afraid of and he'll take extra precautions for you."

"Why don't you and Lydia take off for somewhere—the Fiji Islands? Kreevich has no reason to keep you here. He knows you two are innocent. You can't help. You can't see, for God's sake!"

For just an instant Quist was tempted. "I can hear, I can feel, I can sense what's going on around me," he said. He felt Lydia's fingers tighten on his wrist. He smiled at her. "And I have the loveliest pair of eyes in the world to see for me. I want to be in on this, Max. I have a score to settle with this character."

"I'd give anything to be as free as you are to take off," Marsden said.

"I'm going to get Lydia to take me down where the action is," Quist said. "Sit tight, Max. There's a cop outside the door. Nobody's going to get to you."

"Except the possibility of a friend who's gone crazy," Marsden said.

"Then come with us, Max, stay with us," Quist said.

Marsden waved at a scattering of papers on his desk. "I've got a sea of red ink to face, Julian. When I see how deep it is I may not care what happens to me."

Quist took Lydia's arm as they went out into the hall and down the steps into the theater.

"I thought you were about to tell him you could see," Lydia said, her voice low.

"Poor old guy, it might have helped him," Quist said. "But I couldn't risk his letting it slip to the wrong person."

"You still think someone may make a move, not knowing that you can see? If I'm with you, they'll know you've got eyes to see for you."

"Once we're settled somewhere in the theater you'll leave me," Quist said.

"Julian!"

"That's the way it's going to be, luv. I don't want you in the way of a falling brick."

"No, Julian!"

"I think I can handle myself very well, my darling, especially since no one thinks I can."

The stage was lighted and the company of actors and chorus people were gathered there, listening to something Larry Shields was telling them. The orchestra was in the pit, an occasional tuning sound coming from an instrument. Looking at the strained faces, Quist thought he could almost smell anxiety, hanging over them all like a cloud.

"Before I settle somewhere I want to warn Kreevich about Max's fears," Quist said. He looked around the darkened audience area, but he couldn't see the detective anywhere. "He was going to use Sharon's dressing room to question people. We can go down the side aisle, through the stage box. There's a door at the rear that'll take us backstage."

Moments later they were at the door of Sharon's dressing

154

room. A cop was guarding it. He knew who Quist was, obviously from his "blindness."

"I'll tell the lieutenant you want to see him, Mr. Quist."

The cop went into the dressing room and came back almost at once. He held the door open and gestured Quist and Lydia in. Kreevich was there with a young man in work jeans and shirt.

"This is Tony Baldwin," Kreevich said. "He's the sound designer. Mr. Quist, Miss Morton."

"Hey, I suppose you could say you had it lucky, Mr. Quist," the young man said. "At least you're up and around. This is a crazy business."

"What, may I ask, is a sound designer?" Quist asked.

"The human voice isn't enough for audiences these days," young Baldwin said. "Actors are miked, sound amplifiers all over the house. We try to make it sound human." He grinned. "Anyway, it's created a new kind of job in the theater."

"I was talking with Baldwin because he was friendly with Janet Lane," Kreevich said. "Unfortunately, no kind of lead."

"What a ghastly thing to happen," Baldwin said, his face clouding. "She was a real nice lady, a little long in the tooth for me, but fun to have a drink with. Endless amusing stories about our leading lady."

"Just keep listening, Baldwin, and let me know if you hear anything useful."

"Will do. Good luck to you, Mr. Quist."

Kreevich lifted his hands to his face as the young man left the dressing room. "I'm just about running out of gas and there's an army to talk to," he said.

Quist told his friend about Max Marsden's fears for himself.

"That's not too far out," Kreevich said. "I'll give him extra cover. The trouble with this case is that we're dealing

155

with a screwball whose behavior we can't predict; devious, clever, and without a pattern we've been able to uncover."

"I'm going to station myself out in the theater and just watch," Quist said.

"You're not the only one," Kreevich said. "Your friend Bud Tyler has asked if he can come and watch, too. There's a chance, he thinks, he might recognize someone out of Sharon's past—someone she's forgotten. Big star ignores the lowly extra, doesn't even remember that the person exists. That could produce this kind of revenge pattern."

"A holocaust to pay for a professional snub?"

Kreevich's face had a dark, bitter look to it. "Not any further out than guessing that Zuckermann hired a hit man to kill Billy Lockman for getting people to laugh at him! Let me tell you something, Julian. The average homicide has classical motivation—greed, jealousy, a business rivalry which really comes under greed, to stop someone from blackmailing you in exchange for silence about a crime you've committed. Greed again. But when you're dealing with a psycho you have to expect a massive violence to be triggered by no tangible motive at all. John Hinkley shoots the president in order to attract the attention of a girl he doesn't know! We're dealing with someone who may want nothing more than to get his name in the paper. How better to attract attention than take a swing at a big movie mogul, a great movie star, a big-league race car driver, a famous public relations man? Guessing at motive, in this case, may be a real waste of time." The detective drew a deep breath, "So we just go over these people in the company, one by one, until someone turns up sour."

"I'll be out front watching the rehearsal," Quist said. "You have any idea where Dan Garvey went to?"

"He's taken Janet Lane on as his pet project. He's convinced himself she was coming to Beekman Place to tell you something she wanted you to know before she came to me with it. He thinks she could have chattered to someone

156

about it. People liked her, talked to her. I told him to go ahead."

Kreevich's smile was almost as angry as Dan's "threatening smile." "I envy him."

"Oh?"

"It would be nice to be going after one single case instead of four at the same time," Kreevich said.

Out in the theater nothing formal had started yet. The orchestra was in the pit. The cast, the stage managers, the prop people, the stagehands, the rest of the crew were still onstage. Larry Shields, the director, was down in about the third row of seats, surrounded by Sonny Wertz, the musical director, and Peter Romulus, the choreographer.

Lydia walked up the side aisle with Quist toward the back of the theater. Quist continued his blind act, walking with his hand on Lydia's arm.

"There's your friend Bud Tyler at the back of the house," Lydia said.

Quist had already seen Sharon's ex-husband, sitting in his wheelchair, a black silk mask covering his cruelly scarred face. Tyler waved at them as they came up the aisle.

"Wave back," Quist said to Lydia. "He doesn't know I can see him."

Lydia waved. A moment later they came up to the wheelchair, parked just back of the last row of seats at the orchestra level.

"Hi, you two," Tyler said.

"Kreevich told me you were here," Quist said. "What do you expect to see, Bud?"

The crippled race driver shrugged. "Who knows?" he said. "There are so many people involved here. Someone may tie up with Sharon's past, or poor Janet's."

"Wouldn't Sharon have spotted someone like that long ago, during rehearsals?" Quist asked.

157

If Bud smiled, the mask made it invisible. "Sharon only remembers people who are important to her," he said. "When you're at the top of the ladder you don't pay too much attention to the people who are down below you. It's just possible that there's someone she never really noticed from somewhere in the past."

"Or Janet Lane's past?"

Tyler's head seemed to twitch to one side. "Poor dear Janet," he said. "What a thing to happen to her! A friend in need, you could say. Everybody liked her."

"A friend in need to you?" Quist asked.

Tyler nodded. His hands tightened on the arms of his wheelchair. "In the good times, when I was first married to Sharon, she was, of course, sort of ever-present. Sharon needed her, but she never got in the way or interfered with our privacy. Sometimes, when Sharon was on location somewhere, making a film, Janet wouldn't go with her. She'd stay back at home to take care of mail and other stuff. I don't know if she had instructions from Sharon, but she tried to take care of me—meals at home, a nightcap with me so that I wouldn't feel guilty about drinking alone. A very dear, thoughtful, kind person. When I was hurt— Sharon was making a film in Hollywood—Janet flew from the Coast to the hospital where I was in Carolina. She assured me Sharon would be along in a couple of days, had been in touch with the doctors who'd told her I would survive, even that it might be better for me if she didn't see me the way I looked just then." Tyler hesitated. "I've told you I'd had an anonymous letter from someone informing me that Sharon was having a thing with some big film star. I pleaded with Janet to level with me."

"And she, Sharon's loyal friend, did that?" Quist asked.

"There are no secrets in Hollywood," Tyler said. "Janet could have denied it till she was blue in the face and I'd have known the truth sooner or later. Instead, she tried to explain Sharon to me. She tried to tell me that what Sharon had done, was doing, even, didn't mean that she didn't love me, or that I wasn't all she wanted—when we were together. She told me that if I wouldn't allow separations that Sharon would never look at anyone else. I—I almost believed her. I made up my mind to follow Janet's advice to stay close, to be always available. And then—then one day I looked at my face in the mirror. No woman could ever stay with *that;* no woman could ever make love with *that.*"

"Rough for you," Quist said. He knew what "that" looked like.

"So Sharon came, assured me that she loved me, would stay with me, see me through what was up ahead for me. I knew it wouldn't work and I used her infidelities, as public as if she'd performed them in Macy's window, as grounds for a divorce."

"But she hasn't married again," Lydia said, softly.

"Four times I think she played it for real," Tyler said. "Not with Zuckermann, of course. I'm afraid I think that for her, marriage was like the medicine an alcoholic takes to cure him of his sickness. Perhaps she knows now that there's no cure for her addiction and to hell with trying anything."

Sonny Wertz had moved down to the conductor's spot in the orchestra pit and was tapping on his music rack with his baton. The orchestra played a loud discord. The people on stage stopped chattering and turned front. Larry Shields was standing at his place in the third row.

"You all know what the situation is here," he said. "What we're going to do is to spend the rest of the morning going over the chorus routines for the entire show. So the principals will not be needed till after the lunch break. Then we'll take the show from the top and go straight through to the end. We need to run it once without stopping for anything. So, chorus people—take your places for your first entrance and dance in Act One."

Everyone began to move off stage. Someone was changing the lighting effects from a control booth somewhere high up at the back of the theater.

"I'm going to move down a little way," Quist said, "so I can—so I can hear better." He'd almost blown it by saying "so I can see better." "Care to join me, Bud?"

"Think I'd like to be free to move around, look from different angles," Tyler said.

Quist took Lydia's arm. "Take me down about halfway, will you, luv?"

They walked down the center aisle to the eighth row. Quist sat down in an aisle seat. "Now, Lydia, I want you to go to the office. Tell people what's cooking and stay there, with our staff, until I get in touch with you."

"No!"

"That's the only way I can function with any peace of mind," Quist said. "Please don't argue, Lydia. Just go."

He heard a little choking sound from her, and then she bent down, kissed his cheek, and hurried back up the aisle. The house lights began to dim, and the orchestra began to play what Quist guessed was the overture.

For one panicky moment as the lights dimmed, Quist imagined that his ability to see was fading away again. As a cold chill ran down his spine, the stage area was suddenly brilliantly lighted. His eyes weren't failing him.

A couple of dozen chorus people, not in costume, burst out onto the stage, singing what must be the theme song of the show. "Our clubfooted chorus," Peter Romulus had called them. To Quist they seemed anything but that, alive, vital, full of energy and a projection of a kind of joy. Had he been there to be entertained, Quist felt he would have settled back in his seat with a feeling of anticipation.

Larry Shields stood in the third row watching. Peter Romulus, stood on the very front corner of the stage-left, chewing on the knuckles of a hand, scowling at the dancers. Both men were looking for a perfection that Quist couldn't guess at. Quist himself was looking for a murderer, and didn't know what he could possibly expect to see. He hadn't, he thought, devised any sort of sensible plan of action. He was looking for something out of key, yet he didn't know the show, the people; didn't know enough of Sharon's past to recognize anyone who might be a part of it.

He was suddenly aware that someone had slipped into the seat just behind him.

"Why are you here? Do you expect to hear an irregular heartbeat?" Dan Garvey's sharp voice asked him.

Quist turned. "Dan! Nobody's told you?"

"Told me what?"

"That I can see," Quist said.

Dan's strong hand gripped Quist's shoulder. "My God, Julian! When?"

They spoke in near-whispers to keep from disturbing what was happening onstage. "When I woke up this morning. Only Lydia and Kreevich, and now you, know. We thought that if I kept pretending someone might make a betraying move, thinking I still couldn't see."

"You're not going to see anything here that everyone else won't see," Garvey said. "Can we go to the back of the house where we can talk a little more freely?"

Quist stood up. "Sure, if you'll take my arm and guide me."

Garvey chuckled. "You practicing for an Academy Award?" The two men started back up the aisle toward the darkened rear of the theater. "What the hell is your friend Bud Tyler doing here?" Garvey asked.

"He persuaded Kreevich he might see somebody in the company, actors and crew, who might have some remote connection with Sharon's past."

"You all seem to be obsessed with the idea that you can *see* something. I suppose Tyler might, but you don't know what you're looking for."

161

They reached the back of the house. It was dark in the open area behind the orchestra seats. Looking back toward the front, Quist saw Bud Tyler, huddled in his wheelchair, about halfway down the left-side aisle. Quist turned back to Garvey, and the dark, intense man with the threatening smile, put an arm around him and gave him a gentle hug.

"I was sick with worry for you, chum," Garvey said.

"I've been grateful to you for caring," Quist said. "Kreevich says you've been trying to check up on Janet Lane. Any luck?"

Even in the darkness Quist could see his friend's bright, angry smile. "Only a few things, so far, that might help us guess what she was up to," Garvey said. "I found out where she was living; the Algonquin, which is just a couple of blocks from here. Nobody there had any reason to pay any particular attention to her comings and goings. But the hotel switchboard has a record of her outgoing calls—for which she'd have to be billed. Last night, about nine o'clock, she made a couple of calls to St. Clare's Hospital. Then, in a half-hour period, she made four no-answer calls to your apartment. There was no answer because we'd all gone to the Beaumont to see Sharon. I tried to call St. Clare's for information. So many calls an hour come into their switchboard, there's no way to keep track of them. They had orders to connect no one to the room where you were supposed to be. All they could tell me was that there'd been dozens of calls for you—the ladies and gentlemen of the press, I suppose. It doesn't matter if a man is critically hurt or ill, the reporters must have their story."

"So then she called my place—without any luck. Why, if she thought I was at the hospital?"

"Did she know about Lydia?"

"They didn't meet," Quist said. "I think I may have mentioned that when Sharon came to my place to have dinner with me she found I had a live-in lady and took off. That's

162

how she happened to run into Zuckermann when she did."

"So she thought she might be able to get your lady on the phone. She kept trying and trying and then decided to go over to your place and wait for someone to show."

"Just to inquire about my health?" Quist asked.

"I don't think so, and neither do you," Garvey said. "She had something to tell you, something that had to do with Sharon, or possibly the shot that was taken at you."

"If she had that kind of information, there was always Mark—the police."

"I keep telling myself that," Garvey said. "There was just one person in the world to whom she owed more than a casual loyalty."

"Sharon?"

Garvey nodded. "So she found out something, something that could be damaging to Sharon."

"She'd go to Sharon with it, wouldn't she?"

"Maybe, and we can ask. But you were Sharon's friend, you were not going along with what appeared to be the police theory about Zuckermann's murder, you were a friend of Kreevich's. You might be able to help protect Sharon."

"So she comes to Beekman Place, is mugged before she gets into the building. It had to be before she came in asking for me, Dan. The lobby attendant in my building would have remembered if she'd gotten to the building to ask for me."

"I know. I think she was just going in when she came face to face with someone she knew coming out. The guy couldn't duck her, and so he had to handle her then and there."

"Because he couldn't have her mentioning that she'd seen him at my place?"

"Because he'd planted a bomb in your medicine cabinet," Garvey said. "I don't think Janet could have sus-

163

pected anything. She probably told this guy she knew that she'd come to find you or Lydia to inquire about your condition. This character tells her that's why he's there, too. He's found out there's no one in the apartment, suggests they walk down to the corner bar and have a drink while they wait for someone to show up at your place. She has no reason to suspect he's telling her anything but the truth, agrees, starts to walk away with him. He sees that the street's clear and he doesn't wait. He slugs her, probably with a gun butt, makes sure it's total, snatches her bag so that it will look like an ordinary crime, and hightails it out of there. Now, when the bomb goes off, she won't be around to tell anyone that he was seen at your place."

Quist was silent for a moment. "If what you say is so, then the cop in the lobby, the lobby attendant, the doorman at my place. . . ?"

"I've covered that," Garvey said. "Several strangers left the building. The Weatherbys' party, remember? Guests in other apartments. The cop and the building people had no reason to check on people leaving the place, only strangers coming in."

"They heard Janet scream," Quist said. "That should have set it up in time. Actually the lobby attendant ran out on the street, saw Janet, called the cops."

"But they didn't pay any special attention to anyone leaving just before that. I told myself it was pretty risky for him, having just booby-trapped your place, to come down in one of the front elevators and walk right out through the lobby. Then I realized that was the safest way for him to do it. Try the service elevator at the back, the fire stairs, out through the basement—if he was seen, he'd be stopped, questioned. He came in with a party and he was just leaving a party, if anyone wanted to know. He's home free, and then he walks head-on into Janet."

"It makes sense," Quist said, "but it doesn't give us a notion of who he could be."

164

"I still think Janet had something on her mind that could be harmful to Sharon. She wanted your help. There's just a chance she talked to Sharon. I think we should find her and talk to her."

"We're not supposed to mention the bomb," Quist said.

"Hell, why not? He knows it didn't work. He's seen you walking around here, alive and well."

The gay music, played at a fast rhythm by the brilliant orchestra Sonny Wertz had put together, the vigorous dancing done by the chorus, seemed to belong in some other world than the one that involved murder and plots for violence.

It was Dan Garvey who went looking for Sharon Ladd, who had to be somewhere in the theater, though she wasn't involved with what was happening onstage. Her dressing room was being used as a place for interrogations by Kreevich. There was a greenroom located on the level below the stage where actors could relax during a performance when they weren't personally involved. Garvey, looking there, found it pretty well filled with chorus people not needed for the number being rehearsed onstage. Someone told Garvey she'd heard Sharon say she was going up to Max Marsden's office. She'd be there in case the schedule was changed in some way and Larry Shields wanted her.

Garvey went back up into the orchestra seats of the theater where Quist still waited. "Take my arm and act blind," he said. "Sharon's up in Max's office."

She was there as advertised. Max, sitting at his desk, was bending over some notes, peering at them through a pair of half-glasses. Sharon was perched on the arm of his chair, an arm around his shoulder, looking down at whatever it was the old man was figuring.

"Wrong moment?" Garvey asked.

"No. Welcome, friends," Max said. "How are things going downstairs?"

"Noisy, lively, sounds like fun," Quist said.

"Those kids give it everything when they get turned on," Sharon said.

Max looked up at the beautiful woman sitting on the arm of his chair. "Mind if I tell Julian and Dan what you've been up to?"

"Not such a big something," Sharon said, giving him a warm smile. She swung away from the chair arm and walked across the room.

"Sharon has offered to make a readjustment in our financial deal," Max said.

"Not such a big thing," Sharon said. "I helped get Max into this mess he's in. I've simply told him that I'm willing to forget what he owes me so far and apply it to the future, when we get going on all cylinders, and there are audiences to pay the freight."

"Generous and most helpful," Max said.

"Once we have a hit I'll start bleeding you to death again, darling," Sharon said.

"There aren't too many people in our business who would play it that way," Max said. "You gentlemen came here looking for Sharon, didn't you? If that's the way it is, I'd like to start covering some points I've been neglecting for the past couple of days."

"We're trying to concentrate on Janet Lane," Quist said.

Quist, from behind his dark glasses, saw the little twist of pain that moved on Sharon's face. Max, who had risen from his chair, shook his head from side to side.

"Did you talk to Janet at all, Max, after someone took a shot at me?" Quist asked.

"Julian, everybody connected with the show has been in and out of this office since that happened to you yesterday morning, asking questions. Janet may have been one of them, I don't remember. I mean, I don't remember anything special if I did talk to her."

"She got kind of star billing, didn't she, Max?" Garvey asked. "After all, she'd been involved with Julian just minutes before he was shot."

"Yes, I knew that, and the police took up quite a bit of her time because of that. But you'd know now, wouldn't you, if she came up with anything useful?"

"I think the police would like you both to keep quiet about what I'm about to tell you," Quist said. "Last night, when we were all at the Beaumont visiting with you, Sharon, someone broke into my apartment and planted a bomb in the medicine cabinet in my bathroom. When Lydia and Dan and I got back to Beekman Place, Janet had just been mugged. We didn't know just then who it was—just a woman, outside my apartment building. I was too damned exhausted to even bother to brush my teeth. That was fortunate for me or I might not be here now."

"Julian, this is just not possible to believe!" Sharon said.

"Nonetheless it happened," Quist said. "Now, we have guessed that Janet was coming to my apartment in the hope of seeing someone close to me—Lydia or Dan. We think that she was walking toward the building as someone she knew was just coming out, and they met face to face. That someone had just set the bomb in my apartment, and when it blew, hopefully killing me, Janet would remember that she'd seen this person coming out of the building and his goose would be cooked. So he killed her, making it look like an ordinary street mugging."

"Oh, my God!" Sharon said, her hands raised to her mouth.

"But she couldn't have talked to us about that, Julian," Max Marsden said. "She didn't live to talk to anyone about that."

"I know. That's not what we're after, Max. What we

know is that she'd been trying for some time to reach me, calling the hospital, who wouldn't put through calls to me. Couldn't, in fact, because I was not there. She tried to call my apartment number at least four times from her room in the Algonquin. That's on record. That suggests more than just trying to ask about my physical condition. Dan and I both think that she'd stumbled on something that could be dangerous to you, Sharon—didn't want to go to the police with it till she talked to me; wanted my advice on how to handle some kind of hot potato. So, did she talk to you about anything that was troubling her, that she thought might be threatening you?"

"Oh, my God, Julian, there've been so many crazy things. The world's biggest guessing game has been going on around this place." Sharon's scarlet lips quivered. "Janet would have done anything in the world to protect me from any kind of danger."

"Did she, Sharon? That's the question we're here to ask. Did she?"

Her hands still raised to her face, Sharon bent forward like someone with stomach pains. "You know, Julian, I was under arrest, being held in the hospital unit at the Beaumont. I wasn't allowed to see anyone for social purposes. You and Dan and Lydia were special friends of the lieutenant's. At the end of the day, a little before six o'clock, Mr. Jacquith, our lawyer friend, persuaded the lieutenant to let Janet come to see me. I was entitled to see my friend, secretary, and companion. Janet came, but there was a cop in the room the whole time."

"And?"

"Well, poor Janet was pretty tensed up, as I guess everyone was. There'd been Leon's murder, of which I was suspected, the attack on you just after she'd spent time with you. The cops had grilled her about this. She'd stayed on at the theater after almost everyone else had left, going over

168

the mail you'd asked her to check. Mr. Jacquith got word to her that she could come to see me."

"How?"

"Oh, there were still maintenance people in the theater, maybe someone in the box office. I don't know who took Mr. Jacquith's call. Anyway she was walking out of the theater, dark except for work lights on the stage. As she walked out into the audience area, she heard a man call out to someone, obviously some distance away, 'Hey, Locky, watch it!' She looked around, didn't see anyone, and went on out to the street where she got a taxi and came to the Beaumont."

"So what was special about that?" Dan Garvey asked.

"Everything that could possibly have any bearing on what's been happening," Sharon said. "My third husband's name was Lockman, Billy Lockman. 'Locky,' Janet thought, sounded like a nickname for him."

"But he's been dead for what, four, five years?" Quist asked.

"Almost six. Oh, it sounded hysterical when Janet told me. Some kind of crazy coincidence. Could be someone also named Lockman, or Luckman, or Lockwood—Locky, Lucky. Of course there was no connection with Billy Lockman, but he'd come back into our minds. I'd always believed, and Janet knew it, that Leon Zuckermann was responsible for Billy's death. I believed that, Janet believed it, Bud Tyler, my last husband, believed it. To hear someone call out what might be his name—" Sharon gave a little helpless shrug.

"Janet wasn't actually suggesting she thought Billy had come back from the dead!" Dan Garvey said.

"No, but—"

"But *what?*" Quist asked sharply.

"The Lockmans are a big family," Sharon said. "It seems obvious that someone was out to get Leon and me at the same time. Hearing that name 'Locky' called out, Janet thought some member of Billy's family might have moved in on this company."

"You'd have known him, recognized him, wouldn't you?"

"The Lockmans are a big clan," Sharon said. "I didn't know them all. Billy and I, while we were married, didn't spend much time in Texas."

"That's pretty damn far out," Garvey said.

"It shouldn't be too hard to find out if there's someone in the stage crew, the maintenance people, the chorus who has a nickname that might sound like Locky," Quist said. "Ring a bell with you, Max?"

Max Marsden shook his head. "I wouldn't know the nicknames of any of these people," he said. "We could go over the payroll to see if there's a Lockman, or a Luckman, or a Lockwood. She heard one male voice calling out to this Locky, Sharon?"

"She thought it was someone down in the audience level calling up to someone who was working on lights, high up at the back of the house. Somebody working on equipment somewhere."

"You thought it was something that should worry you?" Quist asked.

"No, I didn't—and I don't," Sharon said. "Janet was on the edge of hysteria. There was a cop there in the hotel hospital listening to what we said. He didn't seem interested. I didn't mention it to the lieutenant or to you because so much else was happening, and it just didn't seem to mean anything."

"Young Thompson, the assistant stage manager who's your friend, would know if there's someone in the crew who has a nickname that might sound like Locky," Quist said. "Let's talk to him."

"He's backstage, working with the chorus right now," Sharon said.

"We'll catch him in a break," Quist said. "Let's go back down into the theater, Dan."

All four of them walked out past the cop in the hallway and down the stairway to the back of the orchestra section of seats. The chorus and orchestra were still going full speed ahead. Quist, glancing down the left-side aisle, saw Bud Tyler still parked in his wheelchair where he'd last seen him. Sharon's fingers closed on his wrist.

"What's Bud doing here?" she asked.

"He thought he might see something that would be useful," Quist said. "Kreevich gave him permission to come and look."

"See what?" Sharon asked.

"Maybe someone out of your past you might have forgotten, or overlooked somehow during the rehearsals."

"That's pretty wild!" Sharon said. "I don't forget people like that! There's no one in this company I've ever worked with before. These are all stage people, not film people."

"Bud and Kreevich both thought there might be a chance."

The orchestra played the last, climactic notes of a number and the action onstage came to an end. Larry Shields was calling out for a fifteen-minute break and for them to return for "the first number in Act Two."

Max Marsden had walked down to talk to his director and after a moment he turned and waved to them. "Thompson will come out and talk to you."

The stage emptied of performers and the musicians crowded out of the orchestra pit. Moments later Tommy Thompson came out through the stage-right box and up the aisle. He stopped for a moment to speak to Bud Tyler and then came to the back of the house where Quist and Sharon and Dan Garvey waited. He smiled at Sharon.

"Your ex-spouse doesn't seem to have come up with anything useful," he said. "I don't quite know what he hoped

171

for, but he hasn't seen anyone who has a connection with your film work, Missy."

"I don't know why everyone thinks I'd have forgotten someone I've worked with," Sharon said.

Thompson turned to Quist. "You wanted me for something?"

"Who is Locky?" Quist asked.

Thompson's eyes narrowed. "Come again," he said.

"Someone in the company or the orchestra or the crew who goes by the name of Locky," Quist said.

Thompson, frowning, shook his head. "That doesn't ring any bell with me. Locky?"

"Or Lucky—something that could have sounded like Locky," Quist said.

"Yesterday afternoon, along about six o'clock, Janet Lane was leaving the theater," Dan Garvey said. "It was dark except for work lights on the stage. She heard someone call out, 'Hey, Locky, watch it!' Who would have been working here in the theater at that time?"

"Yesterday?" Thompson was still frowning, as if it would help him dredge up something. "Everything was haywire here yesterday," he said.

"Janet thought it was someone down in the orchestra seats calling up to someone who might be working on lights," Quist said.

Thompson shook his head. "Normally that would have been time for a rehearsal break," he said, "but there was no rehearsal yesterday. Cops here all day, searching a hundred and fifty people for the gun that was used to shoot at you, Quist, questioning everyone. I was long gone, back to my favorite saloon." He grinned. "It sure was time for a drink. Still cops everywhere you turned." His eyes widened. "Could have been a cop calling to another cop? What's important about it?"

"Probably nothing," Quist said. "Janet was probably all nerves at that time of day. She heard someone call out the

172

name Locky. One of Sharon's ex-husbands was named Billy Lockman."

"But—pardon me, Missy—he's long dead, isn't he?"

"Yes," Quist answered for Sharon. "But Janet knew Zuckermann had been murdered, and someone was out to get Sharon. She thought some other Lockman might have got himself a job somewhere in this operation."

"No Lockman," Thompson said positively. "Unless he's one of the musicians. I don't know them from Adam."

"If we could just find the person Janet heard calling out that name, we could erase this whole fantasy from the blackboard," Quist said.

"I'll try to find out for you," Thompson said. "I still think it may have been cops. They were swarming all over the place."

"At six o'clock?"

"Well, I can't swear to it as an eyewitness," Thompson said. "Like I told you, I'd taken off for a much-needed drink around four-thirty, five o'clock. But some of the maintenance people would have been around. Let me check it out for you."

"Thanks," Quist said.

"Keep your cool, Missy," Thompson said to Sharon. "It's all going to work out okay."

Thompson walked down the aisle, stopped again to speak to Bud Tyler, and then disappeared into the stage box and on backstage.

"Could be like he said," Garvey suggested. "Cops, and Janet didn't hear it quite right. Could have been 'Luke' or 'Lucky.'"

"It would be nice to be able to check it out and write it off," Quist said. "Nagging loose ends—like the woman who phoned the desk at the Beaumont to say she'd heard shooting on the twelfth floor. Why hasn't she come forward? Then we could forget about her."

"Will someone named Rocky, Lucky, Locky, Ducky

173

please step forward?" Garvey said, smiling his angry smile.

There is one thing about a police investigation: it tends to be thorough. Kreevich, too, was trying to track down loose ends. The key used by the person who had substituted drugs for Sharon's sleeping pills had almost certainly been duplicated from the one Sharon carried in her handbag. As Kreevich had suggested earlier, there was a hardware store on Eighth Avenue, not a block and a half from the Tempest Theater where the duplicate could have been made.

The morning rehearsal was about to break when Kreevich came out from backstage and stopped by the aisle seat where Quist had taken up his post.

"The music goes round and round—and comes out nowhere," the detective said. "I'm not good for much more if I don't get some sleep. Sergeant Hanson will be in charge here till I come back. Couple of hours make a new man of me."

Quist told him the "Locky" story.

"One of those damn things you trip over in a case like this," Kreevich said. "It probably doesn't mean anything but you can't let it hang out. I'll have Hanson talk to the cops who were on duty at the time. I don't know any Locky myself. It shouldn't be too hard for Thompson to check out the company and crew."

Kreevich turned to leave as a uniformed cop came down the aisle from the back of the house, accompanied by a dark-haired young man wearing tan slacks and a blue business shirt with the sleeves rolled up to his elbows.

"This is George Markowski, Lieutenant," the cop said. "He works in a hardware store over on Eighth Avenue. He says he made a duplicate key for Sharon Ladd."

"You made it for Miss Ladd?" Kreevich said.

"Well, like for her but not for her," Markowski said. He was obviously frightened.

174

"Try that on again for size," Kreevich said.

"I mean, this young guy came in the shop with this hotel key he wanted copied," Markowski said. "We don't ordinarily copy hotel keys. I mean, you think right away of hotel thieves."

"But you copied it?"

"Well, he told me it was the key to Sharon Ladd's suite at the Beaumont. He said Miss Ladd needed an extra key for her personal maid, I think. Sounded logical enough, and he put a ten-spot down on the counter and just let it lie there."

"A bribe?" Kreevich asked.

"A tip, I figured," Markowski said. "Big-shot stars, people like Sharon Ladd, are pretty generous with tips. I used to moonlight in the hatcheck concessions at a couple of night spots. I've seen some of those Hollywood types tip as much as fifty bucks, just for smiling when you handed a guy his hat."

"So you made the key—for Miss Ladd's maid?"

"Yeah, I made it—and kept the ten-spot!"

"Would you recognize the man who brought you the key?"

"I might. There wasn't anything special about him."

"The company is just breaking now for lunch," Kreevich said. "Everybody will be back here at one o'clock. I want you here then, watching until you see the guy you made the key for."

"They need me at the shop," Markowski said.

"You'll be here," Kreevich said, "or find yourself cooling your heels in a jail cell somewhere."

"I'll be here," Markowski said, as the cop led him away.

"That just might get us moving," Kreevich said. "I guess I'll have to wait for my nap. I want to be here when Markowski spots the guy who had that key made. Could be the ball game."

Quist stayed where he was during the break, going over and over in his mind the few facts they had, trying to make

175

something fit together. Dan Garvey had gone backstage with Tommy Thompson trying to check out on the Locky clue. At a few minutes before one o'clock Larry Shields came out into the audience area. He spotted Quist and came up the aisle to join him.

"I take it nothing has opened up," he said. "I saw your friend Garvey backstage with Tommy Thompson. I never heard of anyone named Locky in the company."

"It's probably meaningless," Quist said.

"It must be rough for you, not being able to see what's going on," Shields said.

"I hope I don't have to find out if it's true," Quist said, "but they say blind people have their other senses sharpened—hearing, sense of smell, instinctive alarms of one kind or another. You're starting the show from the top?"

"After we see about Sharon's entrance," Shields said. "She's supposed to fly in from outer space." Quist could, of course, see the gestures Shields made as he described the entrance. "She comes down a guide wire from the very top of the house at the back, down over the audience, and onto the stage. It's quite spectacular."

"And dangerous?"

"No—not unless the wire broke, which it won't."

"You check it out before each use?"

"After each use," Shields said.

"When did you last use it?"

"About three days, I guess. Things have been so damned hectic around here."

"Just because of that, I suggest you check it out now, before Sharon uses it again," Quist said.

"You don't think—?"

"I don't think you should run even the smallest risk," Quist said.

Shields hesitated, scowling. Then he nodded decisively. "You're right, of course." He turned toward the stage and called out. "Tommy! Tommy Thompson!"

Thompson came out of the wings and down to the footlights.

"I want to check out on Sharon's flying gear," Shields said. "Take one of the stage-crew mechanics along with you."

"We did check it out after the last time, Larry," Thompson called out.

"All the same, check it now, Tommy."

"You got it," Thompson said, and disappeared backstage.

Shields turned to Quist. "Thompson knows this equipment inside out, helped design it," he said. "But I have to send a second man with him. Unions! I want to move a chair on the set, it has to be a stagehand. I can't ask an actor to do it. Something mechanical, it has to be handled by a special union man, not the guy who knows the most about it."

The members of the orchestra were beginning to file into the pit and the tuning-up process was beginning. Quist, anxious to see where Thompson and his mechanic were going, got up and walked toward the back of the house, going through the charade of touching the back of each seat as he moved. He could see the wire, and the little platform high up above the second balcony near the ceiling. He caught a glimpse of Sharon up there, and then Thompson and another man came into plain view. At the back of the house Bud Tyler had moved his wheelchair to the top of the aisle.

"What's cooking, Quist? It's Tyler."

"They're checking the rigging that Sharon uses to make her entrance."

"Oh," Tyler said in a flat voice.

"Extra precautions," Quist said.

A voice was shouting down from the sky-high platform. Quist couldn't make out the words from under the overhanging balcony, but he could see Larry Shields shouting back, waving.

177

"Something wrong?" Tyler asked.

"Looks like it."

Actors were crowding out on stage, looking up. Shields came partway up the aisle. "Sharon owes you, we all owe you, Julian. She could have broken her lovely neck!"

A few minutes later Tommy Thompson came down the stairway from behind where Quist and Tyler were located. The assistant stage manager's face was white, strained-looking.

"Sabotage," he said. "Someone loosened the bolts that hold the wire. If Sharon had started down she would have crashed down onto the seats." Thompson was staring straight at Quist. And then he did something that Quist would never forget. He reached out a hand and waved it directly in front of Quist's dark glasses. It was so unexpected that only a miracle of self-control kept Quist from flinching. *Thompson was trying to make certain that Quist couldn't see!* He went on talking, something about the bolts having been loosened, just hanging by a thread. But as he spoke, he was making a signal to Tyler for silence. From the pocket of his work jacket Thompson took a handgun and passed it over to Tyler, who promptly slipped it under the robe that covered his crippled legs.

"I got to give the bad news to Larry, and the cops, I suppose," Thompson said. He started walking down the aisle.

"My god," Tyler said. "Somebody really is after Sharon."

Quist didn't recognize the sound of his own voice. "Someone like you and Thompson?" he asked.

As Tyler started to fumble under his lap robe, Quist grabbed the back of the wheelchair and started pushing it ahead of him, at breakneck speed, down the aisle and toward Shields and the assembled company. Tyler's reflexes were what Quist had hoped they would be. He couldn't fumble for the gun, he had to hold onto the arms of the

178

wheelchair to save himself in the dizzying race down the aisle toward the orchestra pit. Someone on stage screamed as Quist smashed the wheelchair into the iron railing that separated the front-row seats from the orchestra pit. Tyler catapulted forward, but was trapped between the rail and the back of the chair. Quist, winded by the impact of the crash, was reaching around from behind Tyler, searching for the gun. Someone had him by the shoulders, trying to pull him away.

"You gone crazy, Julian?" It was Dan Garvey.

"He's got a gun under that robe!"

Garvey made a dive at Tyler, who was doubled over the orchestra-pit railing. Suddenly Sharon was there, clinging to Quist.

"What's happening, Julian? The man's a cripple!"

"*Quist!*" It was a loud shout, thunderously loud, coming through the amplifiers in the theater. Quist spun around, Sharon still holding onto him. Standing in the stage box to the left of the stage itself was Thompson. He was holding a stage microphone in one hand, and a handgun in the other.

"Turns out you can see!" Thompson's voice came booming through the speakers. "You had me fooled, Buster. Maybe it's all for the best, because now you can see what's coming."

He raised his gun hand and started to bring it down in a level aim at Quist and Sharon. Quist gave Sharon a violent shove away from him—and heard the sharp report of a gunshot. He turned back toward the stage box, expecting pain to come with shattering force. Instead he saw Thompson fall backward, trip over a chair, and disappear from view.

Standing on stage, just to the right of the box, was Kreevich, slowly lowering his Police Special.

"Don't draw it as fine as that too many times, Julian," the detective said in his cold, flat voice.

Quist heard another voice, low and shaken, speak from just behind him. "Oh, Locky, you damned fool!" Bud Tyler said.

It seemed like centuries later. Actually it was only a few hours. Quist and Lydia and Dan Garvey, along with Sharon Ladd, were sitting on the terrace of Quist's Beekman Place apartment when Kreevich arrived. The detective looked better than he had a few hours back. He'd managed to find time to shave and change into some fresh clothes. It seemed unlikely he could have found time for his nap.

"There are, at least, some facts. Some of them will be painful for you, Miss Ladd, I'm afraid."

"Can there be anything else?" Sharon asked.

"To start with, the man you've known as Tommy Thompson was, in fact, once your brother-in-law. His real name was Thomas Lockman."

Sharon sat up very straight in her chair. "I don't believe it!" she said.

"It puzzled me at first, when Tyler told us," Kreevich said. "How could he be here, working right next to you, taking you to a doctor, directing your comings and goings backstage, and you not recognize him?"

"I never knew him! I never met Billy's brother!"

"I know that now," Kreevich said. "He was a pilot in the Air Force in Germany when you married Billy Lockman. In the year that you and Billy Lockman were together he never came home. Did you never see any pictures of him?"

"There were pictures of Lockmans all over the Texas house," Sharon said. "I wasn't there much, always working on a film. I wasn't particularly interested in the Lockmans, except Billy—for a rather short time, I'm afraid."

"Well, that's who Thompson was. When Billy Lockman was murdered in a Texas saloon, Tom Lockman got himself discharged from the service and came home. He and Billy

180

had been very close. There was the suspicion that Leon Zuckermann had hired a hit man to kill Billy. All Tom Lockman wanted was revenge, revenge on Zuckermann and revenge on you, Miss Ladd. In his twisted mind, Tom told himself that if Billy had never encountered you, he'd have been alive and well. He didn't want something quick. He wanted it to be slow, and painful, and unbearable."

"My God!" Sharon said. "He told you that?"

"He didn't tell me anything, nor will he," Kreevich said. "I don't miss when the pressure is on. It was him, or you and Julian. What I know has come from Bud Tyler."

"Bud knew?"

"He not only knew, I'm sorry to tell you, but two sick minds got together in a plot to destroy you. You were to fail in your show, be publicly ridiculed, and then, when you knew who was responsible, you would have died."

Sharon lowered her head and covered her face with her hands.

"All of Tyler's talk about how much he loved you, would always love you, and wanted to help you, was a cover. Tom Lockman took time to prepare himself, worked in a couple of West Coast theaters, became efficient enough to serve as a stage manager. When you signed up for *Queen Bee,* Miss Ladd, he used some influence he had to get the job of assistant stage manager on your show. He was in business."

"He knew Tyler?" Quist heard himself ask.

"He looked Tyler up because he wanted intimate details about your private life. He found another cesspool of hatred as deep and rotten as his own. They began to scheme together. Incidently, Markowski, the hardware store man, identified Thompson's body as that of the man who'd had the duplicate key to your hotel suite made. And so Thompson—Lockman was able to get into your suite and substitute drugs for your Seconal capsules. You started to come apart. That was fine, exactly the way they wanted it.

181

They began sending messages to Zuckermann—you were falling on your face in rehearsals, Miss Ladd."

"Why?" Dan Garvey asked.

"They wanted him here. They had some plan to deal with you both together. But fate played a hand. Zuckermann arrived and ran into you in the Beaumont lobby, Miss Ladd. Tom Lockman was there. He'd just been to your suite to replenish the supply of drugs he was feeding you. He saw the whole thing in the lobby and he saw a way to really hook you—and Zuckermann. He consulted with Tyler, waited a couple of hours, went back to the hotel and let himself into your room. You were asleep, drugged. Your gun was on the bedside table, as Tyler had told him it would be. He took it, went down to Zuckermann's suite, got himself admitted, and murdered the man he was certain had been responsible for Billy Lockman's murder. Then he went back to your room and replaced the gun and took off."

"The woman who called the desk about hearing the shots in Zuckermann's suite?" Quist asked.

"We don't know. Tyler says it wasn't a part of their scheme. It could have been someone just passing by the open door who didn't want to get involved. It could have been a woman Zuckermann was entertaining who didn't dare get involved. It doesn't matter much now. At the time Tyler and Tom Lockman thought they'd pulled off the perfect finale. Zuckermann was dead and you, Miss Ladd, would be prosecuted and convicted for the murder. Then you got in the way, Julian."

"By not buying what they had to sell?"

"Right. They were both way out over the deep end. They had the perfect result for all their planning, provided Sharon was held for murder. You, Julian, went to the theater with all your doubts about it. Thompson may have heard you talking to Max Marsden, or Janet Lane, or someone.

You were danger. When you left the theater Thompson–Lockman was waiting out in the crowd for you. He missed you by a fraction of an inch."

"All they had to do was stay quiet and they were in the clear," Dan Garvey said.

"Sick, sick, sick," Kreevich said. "If Miss Ladd didn't get it one way, she was going to get it another. Tyler, in the theater with my permission, God forgive me, was waiting for Tom Lockman to sabotage that flying gadget so that Miss Ladd would crash down to her death when she next used it. They thought the theater was deserted, when Janet Lane appeared from backstage. That's when Tyler called out to his ally, 'Hey, Locky, watch it!'"

"So Janet did hear what she thought she heard?" Quist asked.

"But that isn't what did for her," Kreevich said. "Those two madmen didn't give up. You had to be silenced for keeps, Julian. They couldn't get at you at the hospital, but sooner or later you would come home. Thompson–Lockman came here to Beekman Place, waited till he could go in unnoticed—in the Weatherby party—got to your floor, found a way in. You shouldn't blame yourself for the unlocked kitchen door, Lydia. He'd have forced it if he'd had to. He set the bomb, went out the way he'd come, and walked into Janet just outside the building. He was done for. When the bomb went off she'd remember seeing him. And so—poor Janet Lane."

"Oh, God!" Sharon whispered.

"They were both legitimately in the theater today," Kreevich said. "Thompson–Lockman at his job: Tyler, with my permission again, to look for someone he might know. He wasn't there for that. He was there to witness the final climax, and to weep his crocodile tears for us after it happened."

"Final climax?" Garvey asked.

183

"Miss Ladd would be rehearsing her flying sequence and go crashing down to her death in the middle of the orchestra seats. Thanks to Julian's anxiety for you, Miss Ladd, that never happened."

"You know what's the most remarkable thing?" Quist asked after a moment of silence. "That I didn't flinch when Thompson–Lockman waved his hands in front of my eyes. I saw him pass the gun to Tyler. Why that, Mark?"

"Those two sick men thought they might have to shoot their way out. The theater and the company had been searched for guns. Thompson–Lockman got two guns somewhere and passed one to his partner in front of a blind man."

"That crazy run down the aisle with the wheelchair, Julian?" Garvey asked.

"He had the gun in his hand under that lap robe," Quist said. "I figured he was off his rocker. If I tried to take it from him I might have gotten the works. I thought if I raced him down the aisle he'd have to drop the gun and hang on."

"Thank God it worked," Lydia said.

"There's one big hole in all of this, Mark," Quist said. "Did Zuckermann arrange for the murder of Billy Lockman and the wrecking of Tyler's car?"

"Still to be proved," Kreevich said, "but I believe with Miss Ladd that he did. And created two maniacs in the process."

"What will happen to Bud?" Sharon asked.

"We live under some very strange laws, Miss Ladd," Kreevich said. "He may get off on grounds of insanity. God knows he's insane. Hopefully he will be behind bars in a mental institution."

Quist reached out and took Lydia's cold hand in his. "I think it's time for something like a triple nightcap," he said.